BURT & MULLET
KID DETECTIVES

THE PEANUT BUTTER THIEF

C.E. AUSTIN

Copyright ©2023 C.E. Austin
Published by Doorway Publishing

All rights reserved. No portion of this book may be reproduced in any form without permission, except for brief quotations in critical reviews or articles, without prior written permission of the author.

This is a work of fiction. Any resemblance to actual events, locales, or persons, living or dead, is entirely coincidental.

ISBN: 978-1-954771-17-8

Cover Design: Jakki Jelene

Published in the United States of America

Dedication:

For Hannah, the funniest, prettiest, and most kind-hearted peanut butter thief I know.

—Chapter 1—
THE TRYOUTS

Please call my name. Please call my name. Maybe if he thought it enough times, he could force it to happen. There were only three spots left, and Burt wanted to hear his name called out more than anything in the entire world.

Coach Clay flipped the page on the clipboard and paused. Burt squeezed his palms so hard against the bleachers that he thought he might leave indents on the metal.

"The next person to make the elite summer all-star team is..." Coach Clay paused for what felt like forever, causing Burt's heart to pound so hard, that he could hear the thumps thundering in his ears.

"Burt Lawrence."

Burt released the breath he had been holding. This year he'd actually done it, he actually made the summer all-star basketball team.

One of the moms behind him clicked her tongue. He wanted to turn and see who it came from, but he forced himself to keep looking forward. Boys from Burt's side of town weren't supposed to make the team. It didn't matter now though, he would show them and their clicking tongues.

His mom nudged him, "Good job, sweetheart, I'm so proud of you."

"Thanks," Burt said as he glanced to his right, where his best friend, Mullet, was sitting.

Mullet's normally tan face suddenly looked whiter than a sheet. The only thing that could ruin this moment is if Mullet didn't make the team with him. For the last two years, they lived and breathed basketball together. First, they played on the Red Pine Elementary fourth-grade league, then the fifth-grade league. When they heard of the summer all-star team, they spent countless hours in Burt's driveway practicing for the tryouts. Last summer neither of them made the team, but this year was going to be different. They worked harder than ever, and they had to make it together… they just had to.

"You're way faster than me and better at layups, so if I made it, you'll make it," Burt said, trying to convince himself as much as he was trying to convince Mullet. His summer would end right then and there if Mullet's name wasn't called too.

Mullet's face pulled into a frown. "There's ten more kids sitting here, and only two spots left. I've only got a twenty-percent chance."

It was just like Mullet to bring up some sort of math. When Burt didn't say anything, Mullet continued. "That means the odds are against me."

"You'll beat the odds," Burt said as someone tapped him on the shoulder. Burt turned to find his mom giving him "the look", and she put her finger to her lips and pointed at the coach.

"The next boy to make the elite summer all-star team is… Peter Gunn."

A few seats over, Peter stood up and threw his hands up in the air like he'd just won the NBA championships or something. Burt didn't know what the excitement was about. Everyone already knew that he would make it. He was from the right part of town, wore the right clothes, and always knew the right thing to say… at least, in front of the adults.

Once everyone settled down from their Peter Gunn fan party, Coach Clay continued. "That leaves one space left on our elite team," Coach Clay said, "Now, I want to remind you that if you don't make the team this summer, it doesn't mean you're not a good player. There was a lot of talent out here and everyone did a great job."

The lecture droned on and on. Burt lost track of what the coach was saying as he stared at the white sock protruding from the pinky toe of his shoe. Between the humid weather and vigorous tryouts, some of the duct tape was coming loose and his shoes were falling apart again. He would make sure to fix them before summer practices started.

Suddenly Mullet's mom jumped up and started screaming, nearly giving Burt a heart attack. She leaned forward and squeezed Mullet so hard that Burt thought his head might pop off.

When Burt realized why she was screaming, he jumped up and squeezed Mullet too. They had done it! They had both made the coveted summer all-star team!

"I told you that you would beat the odds," Burt said as he grinned at his friend.

The coach cleared his throat and Mullet's mom sat down. Apparently, Peter Gunn was allowed to have a loud obnoxious fan club, but Mullet was not.

"That was our last available spot. If you made the team, I will need you to stay here for another few moments. To everyone else, thank you for trying out. Don't give up. Keep playing and make sure to look into the rec league that will start at the community park next week."

And with that, chaos ensued as angry mothers stalked up to the coach, reprimanding and questioning him because their poor little darlings didn't make the team, even though the mothers knew their sweeties were the most talented ones out there. Some glared at him and others grabbed their boys' hands and rushed off toward their vehicles.

A few walked by Burt and Mullet, looking down their prissy noses and sniffing haughtily at them.

"You have every right to be here and be on this team," Mullet's mom said from behind them, "Don't pay any attention to them."

"Alright everyone, I will have Peter pass out the information packets with everything you need to know about this league. As you know, this elite team is the best of the best of the incoming sixth graders from our area. They will get to play games against other counties and will finish with the statewide summer tournament in July. Official practice begins Monday evening, and practices will run on Mondays, Tuesdays, and Thursdays throughout the summer. Games will be on Saturday and Sunday afternoons, and tournaments will be all weekend. You must purchase the team jerseys and shorts. Everything else is recommended, but not required. I'll finish talking with the parents, while the boys go with Peter."

Peter Gunn strutted to the center of the court, chin up in the air and chest puffed out. He was tall for a soon-to-be sixth grader, tan, blonde, and the girls drooled over him. He knew it and might as well had a banner over his head that said, "I think I'm special".

"Bring it in!" Peter yelled and the other guys whooped as they jumped up and circled around him. Burt and Mullet stood at the edge of the group, waiting for Peter to start talking.

"Alright guys, it's our job to choose our team colors for the uniforms. I know what I want, but I'm supposed to ask the team."

"Definitely light blue and white," Mark said, "The limited edition of the SkyScraper Pros comes out this week and since we're all getting them for the league, they need to match our uniforms."

"Totally my thoughts. That's decided then," Peter said without taking a vote or asking anyone else what they thought. "We'll do white uniforms with light blue and everyone needs to get the shoes when they come out next week." Peter's eyes glanced down toward Burt and Mullet's feet as he said this.

Burt and Mullet exchanged horrified glances. Surely not everyone on the team was getting the new SkyScraper Pros, because if that was true, they were doomed.

"Alright, blue on three!" Peter yelled, "One, two, three!"

"Blue!" Everyone shouted and then took off.

Burt and Mullet grabbed their bags and walked towards Burt's minivan, where their moms were waiting in the air conditioning.

"Mullet, what's the chance of us getting those shoes?" Burt said as he swung his sports bag over his shoulder.

"In my professional opinion, I'd say definitely zero percent."

"Think we can beat the odds two times in one day?"

"Not a chance," Mullet said.

As they walked up, they could see their moms reading through the parent information packets. It was now or never.

"Mom, the team just talked and everyone is getting new shoes for the basketball team. Can we get new shoes too?" Burt said as he climbed into the back of the van. By the look on his mom's face, maybe he should have went with never.

"That was brave," Mullet whispered from behind him.

Both moms were silent as they buckled their seatbelts. That was never a good sign.

"The coach said that new shoes weren't necessary to play on the team and I just confirmed that in the packet. The only things we are required to buy are the shorts and the uniforms," his mom finally said.

"Mom?" Mullet said, giving his luck a try as he leaned forward, "The whole team is getting the new SkyScraper Pros. They're even making our uniforms blue and white to match them."

"Hold on a second, aren't those the shoes that everyone is talking about because they are the most expensive basketball shoes to come out on the market?" Burt's mom said.

"I really dislike those silver spoons," Mullet's mom mumbled under her breath.

"Andrea," Burt's mom gasped.

"They always have to have the best and newest of everything, and now they got our kids thinking that too. Those silver spoons always leave a bad taste in my mouth and they should for you too."

It made Burt's day when Mullet's mom referred to the rich kids as the silver spoons. He didn't blame her. She endured plenty of looks and taunts from them at the library where she worked. His parents didn't allow him to use her nickname for them, but he and Mullet always did.

They lived in the old part of Red Pine, which consisted of older homes in the neighborhood. It was described as quaint, but was nothing like the new side of town, with its ritzy country club, golf courses, and immaculate houses the size of mansions.

Burt noticed his mother's hands tighten across the steering wheel as she guided them out of the parking lot. She looked into her rearview mirror and caught his eye. "Burt, you know how it is. This league will be expensive enough for us without adding brand new shoes on top of it. There's uniforms, traveling to the games, paying for food, admission, gas… I mean it goes on and on. We're happy to be a part of it, but that doesn't mean we can afford everything."

He shot a sideways look to Mullet as she buzzed on about expenses with Mullet's mom nodding beside her.

"Burt, are you listening to me? You'll get a new pair this fall for your school basketball season and that's final. Besides, we just bought you nice basketball shoes last winter for the fifth-grade league. You can make those work."

"But those were fifth-grade shoes," he said as he looked at Mullet and then looked down at his shoes. They both knew what he meant, shoes for babies that were too bright and too lame for the summer season. Besides, they spent so much time running, jumping, and pivoting in those things that they were literally in pieces. If it wasn't for the discarded collection of crazy-colored duct tape that he'd found in his sister's closet, neither his nor Mullet's shoes would probably stay on their feet. Didn't she realize what it was like to wear duct-taped shoes around the silver spoon kids?

Besides, if Burt and Mullet had any chance at surviving the season at all, they had to get the new Skyscrapers just like everyone else. It wasn't an option not to have them, even if the coach said they "weren't mandatory". If the kids in their own town, on their own team, made fun of them, just imagine what the guys from the other teams would think. Burt could picture it now.

"Did you steal those shoes from your baby brother?"

"Wow, they pick you guys up on the side of the road?"

Nope, they would never live it down. Never. If his parents weren't going to get him the shoes, he'd have to find a way to get the shoes himself.

—Chapter 2—
LEMONADE SALE

"Whoever came up with the idea of a lemonade stand wasn't trying to make millions," Burt said as he pushed his light blonde hair out of his face and watched the neighborhood houses with disbelief. He stared down the forlorn street and slumped back into his chair.

Mullet emptied the jar to count the money. Mullet *always* went by his last name... *always*. Burt watched with nervousness as Mullet counted the change a second time, his eyebrows furrowing together as he did the math.

So much for getting rich and striking it big. They were short three cents, but Burt had been too afraid to tell Mullet. The meltdown was coming and he needed to brace himself.

"There's only ninety-seven cents here," Mullet said as he attempted to balance the jar on his knee and frowned up at Burt.

"I know," Burt said, watching the jar teeter back and forth until Mullet caught it and eyed him suspiciously.

"You realize that's impossible, right? We sell our lemonade for twenty-five cents a cup, so we should have fifty cents or seventy-five cents or a dollar. C'mon Burt, with the price we set, our totals should always end in a zero or a five. Hence the "seven" in ninety-seven doesn't work. We're three cents short!" Mullet said as he shook the jar, the change clinking adamantly as he spoke.

Taking a deep breath, Burt grabbed the jar away from him and set it steadily on the table. If selling lemonade was a sport, they would definitely get benched. Somehow, they had imagined selling hundreds and hundreds of glasses of lemonade when they set up their stand, but all they had to show for it so far was a few coins, sunburned noses, and negative three cents.

He could feel Mullet's eyes boring into him and figured he had better just get it over with.

"Oh, alright!" he said, throwing his hands up. "Old man Langley stopped by earlier and he only had twenty-two cents with him. He said he miscounted before he left home, and went on and on about how thirsty he was, so I told him he could just have it for twenty-two cents."

"You told him it was fine and you didn't think to consult me about it first? *Your* business partner? He probably just made that whole story up, because he's a rickety old cheapskate!" Mullet said as he slammed his fist on the table. The jar wobbled back and forth and finally settled, but Mullet looked anything but settled.

"How was I supposed to consult you? You were in the bathroom!" Burt shot back.

"We haven't even made a dollar yet, because you decided to give old man Langley a discount! There's not even enough to buy a candy bar, let alone the basketball shoes!" Mullet yelled. His cheeks turned the brightest shade of red and Burt was worried his friend was about to have a major breakdown. Not good, considering it was already eighty degrees and humid outside. Normally they were closer than brothers, but they were used to winning. Now the pressure of looming failure and not surviving the sixth grade was tearing them apart.

"Listen, Mullet, Old man Langley looks like he's about to die when he's just sitting on his porch. By the time he got himself out of his chair and walked over here, I thought I was going to have to do CPR or call 911. I couldn't send him back home for three cents, I would have sent him to his death bed," Burt said coolly.

Mullet stood so quickly that his chair tipped over. His small figure seemed to grow the angrier he got and his dark black hair fell over his eyes. He pointed a finger at Burt and shook it in his face. "Go ahead then, give away all the lemonade if you want! We'll never be able to get the shoes by the tournament anyways!" he said as he pivoted around and stormed back to his house.

Burt watched him disappear through the front door and slam it shut with extra oomph. Great, now he was completely alone. No best friend. No business partner. No customers. And no money for shoes. Life over.

He slumped in his chair and pulled out the sweaty magazine ad from his pocket. It was worn with creases from folding it and unfolding it so many times. There they were, the special edition Skyscraper Pro basketball shoes. The shoes that every guy on the team would soon have, everyone except for him and Mullet.

Every minute, from when the sun touched the ground to when it finally disappeared at night, was spent playing basketball. It was everything to them, and the fact that they even showed their faces at tryouts was a huge deal. Now that they had actually made the silver spoons' exclusive basketball team, they should be excited. Those were the boys that could afford swanky summer camps, the best equipment, and the most expensive shoes. Guys like Burt and Mullet never made the team.

At tryouts, the silver spoons made it clear that Burt and Mullet weren't welcome on their turf. They kept making fun of them… and pointing at their shoes. But Burt and Mullet put on a show. Burt rarely missed a three-point shot, and his great post moves made him stand out. Mullet may be small, but his quick speed and ability to read his opponents' moves made him almost impossible to guard. He held the elementary school record for layups, and he didn't disappoint when it came to tryouts.

But as awesome as it was to make the team, every practice would be filled with humiliation. Everything the other guys wore was name-brand, while Burt and Mullet were stuck with thin t-shirts with holes in the armpits and basketball shoes held together with his sister's girly duct tape.

Their penny-pinching moms made it worse by refusing to buy them new shoes for the summer league. They just didn't get it.

"Excuse me," a little voice said.

Burt looked up to see their neighbor, Tiana, standing there holding out a quarter. "Can I get some lemonade?"

"Sure," Burt said as he poured her a glass. Normally she was the chattiest kid in the second grade, but now she was acting almost shy. He traded her the lemonade for the quarter and she skipped away.

Leaning back in his chair, he recounted the conversation from the night before, where both moms had teamed up against them. No matter how much they tried, their moms wouldn't budge on the shoes.

Burt's mom didn't believe in allowances, she believed kids should do work because they're part of the family, and she didn't waste money on frivolous expenses, like new basketball shoes. Her theory was that kids don't get money, they earn it. In fact, she was such a penny pincher that she could spend an entire day turning the whole house upside down searching for a missing dollar.

Mullet's mom was supposed to give him an allowance, but after his father passed away, she kept forgetting to give it to him. He felt too guilty to mention anything to her about it because he knew she struggled to make enough as it was.

So, they were on their own, and together they had conjured up the greatest plan on the planet. They would sell lemonade to the multitudes and make bucketloads of cash. It took two days for their great lemonade-selling dreams to die a hard death.

Burt heard footsteps and turned.

"It's just me," Mullet said. He caught sight of the rumpled ad and gazed at it. "You know, tomorrow is Saturday, I bet lots of people will be around then." He picked up the ad and handed it back to Burt. "Sorry about earlier."

Burt shrugged. "All I can think about is showing up to the first practice and facing those silver spoons. If we at least had those shoes, it would keep their mouths shut." He lifted the ad and stared at Toody Bills, the greatest player in the country. Toody's muscular legs stood out against the sky blue backdrop as he dunked the ball into a basketball hoop made out of clouds. He wore the new white Skyscrapers with their famous light blue insignia. The ad read, "Skyscrapers. Jump so high, you can reach the sky!"

"If only we could be like him," Burt said, his chest tightening as he folded the picture back up and shoved it in his pocket.

"Yeah, forty-six point five points per game, ninety-five percent from the three, fifty-one inch vertical, and leads the league in assists. If we had those shoes, we could do it all," said Mullet.

Burt didn't feel very positive at all. There was no way they were going to make the amount of money they needed by the tournament. At the rate they were going, they wouldn't make enough by next summer…or the following summer. By then it wouldn't matter anymore, because they would already be the laughingstock of the whole middle school.

He should have felt happier, he'd made the team and he made it with his best friend, so it should have been enough. "Maybe you're right. Maybe we'll make loads of money tomorrow."

"Yeah…tomorrow," Mullet said glumly.

"Let's forget about this," Burt said as he stood and started packing up the cups. He grabbed the lemonade and headed towards the refrigerator in the garage as Mullet dragged the chairs behind him. They both carried the table up by Burt's house.

Mullet grabbed the threadbare basketball laying on the ground and threw it at Burt. "Basketball always makes everything better."

Burt grinned, "Yeah, especially when I beat you!" He juked to the left, then to the right, and leapt, taking the basketball in for a layup.

—Chapter 3—
DARCY

The most beautiful sound in the world filled the air, the clink of change jingling in their jar. Apparently, Mullet was right. Saturday was a pretty good day for selling lemonade after all.

A few hours earlier, a carpool mom with a van full of screaming kids drove by and practically swerved into Burt's driveway. She bought seven cups of lemonade for the kids dying of thirst in the backseat. She even gave them a one-dollar tip as she mumbled something about buying her sanity.

After that, a group of elderly ladies walking along the park trail by Mullet's house noticed the sign and turned in their direction. They claimed to be the local walking club, but everyone in town knew that they were really the local gossip club. Hopefully, they would gossip about their great lemonade and get the rest of the town to show up. Until then, Burt did his best to withstand them pinching his cheeks without cringing.

The cheek pinching was worth enduring though, because the old ladies ended up adding extra tips to the jar.

Even old Langley hobbled over from his front porch and bought a glass. He gave them a handful of pennies, claiming there was plenty extra to make up for the day before. They insisted that it wasn't a big deal, but he wouldn't hear of it. Later when they counted, they realized there were only two extra pennies, so he was still a penny short.

"I'll start counting the rest of the money while there's a lull in our sales," Mullet said as he dumped the contents of the jar on the table and started counting the coins one by one.

Burt settled back in his chair with his hands behind his head as he looked around their block. They called it Park End, because the dead end butted up to the walking trail that led to the community park.

No one on their road was necessarily poor, but no one was rich either. The street was filled with normal people, living in normal houses, working normal jobs. There were a couple of teachers, a firefighter, Ben the grocer, and Mullet's mom, the local librarian. Burt's mom stayed home, and his father was a truck driver. Most everyone kept their houses and lawns looking nice. That is, everyone besides Old Langley. The old scarecrow was too old to keep up on it, but too stubborn to let anyone do anything for him. There weren't a lot of kids Burt and Mullet's age, but lots of younger kids. He had to admit it was pretty nice to live on this block, especially since their backyards practically bordered the park.

"Twenty- one, twenty-two, twenty-three," Mullet counted as he slid the coins to the side.

The pile of coins looked meager stacked up in little rows. Although it seemed like they had sold a lot of lemonade, the money didn't add up as fast as Burt thought it would.

Light footsteps pattered down the sidewalk and Burt looked up to see who was coming. He groaned. It was Darcy Bell. Burt quickly looked down at his knees, pretending not to see her.

Darcy's family was the only one that didn't belong on the block. She wasn't really one of them; she was one of the silver spoons. She had always lived on the other side of town and then a month ago, her family moved into the house a few doors down from Burt. Darcy acted like she was too important for this side of town, and Burt wished that she would take her rich family and her snotty attitude, and move back to where she came from.

Whenever they were near each other, they made sure to avoid eye contact. It was an unsaid rule to completely ignore each other at school. What was interesting was that she moved to Park End during spring break, but spent the end of the school year pretending like she'd never moved to their side of town at all. It was like no one knew.

"She better not come over here, or I'll lose it," Mullet said as he glanced up, cringed, and went back to counting the money.

Burt picked at the calluses on his hands, suddenly very intent on getting all the yellowing skin pulled off the top of them. Squishing dead skin between his fingers was way better than talking to Darcy Bell.

"Lemonade?" her shrill voice questioned from a few feet away.

Burt lifted his eyes carefully. He hadn't decided if it was safe or not to let Darcy know that he'd noticed her. She stood in front of their homemade sign, her brown hair tied back with a frilly bow that matched her purple sundress. Who would wear a dress on a Saturday? Didn't she play outside?

Suddenly she looked up and, breaking the rules of their code, made eye contact with him.

"Did you make it from lemons or did you use that powder stuff?" she sniffed.

"Powdered stuff," Burt said flatly, hoping that would send her on her way. Surely, she knew she wasn't supposed to be talking to them.

"Alright then, I'll take some," she said as she unzipped the metallic pink change pouch on her wrist. All the girls at school started wearing them this spring and drove the teachers crazy constantly zipping and unzipping them to pull out fruity lip gloss, money, sparkly hair ties, and whatever other weird things they managed to stuff in there.

"I actually prefer the powdered stuff because it's highly difficult for most people to get the ratio of sweet and sour right when they try to make their own lemonade," she said.

"I don't even know what that means," Mullet whispered to Burt as she walked up to their lemonade stand and dropped a quarter on the table.

They both gawked at her.

"Hurry up," she said, snapping her fingers at them and holding out her hand.

Mullet poured the lemonade with shaky hands as Burt fidgeted. He stared at the quarter without picking it up, wondering if he should even think about touching something that Darcy Bell had just touched.

Mullet shook the pitcher, emptying the last few drops of lemonade into it. It filled the glass just over halfway, and Mullet, who either didn't notice or didn't care, shoved the partially filled glass toward her.

"Thank you for your business and please come again," Mullet said in such a fake friendly voice that Burt almost doubled over with laughter.

Darcy took the glass and held it up. "Is this all that you're going to give me?" she asked.

"That's the last of it," Mullet said.

Burt nodded in support of his friend. If it would have been anyone besides Darcy Bell, he might have gone to the trouble to make more, but unfortunately for her… it was her.

"But there's not even a full glass," she said as she held it up and stared at it.

"As my mom would say, 'Wow, look at that, your glass is half full,' " Mullet said, mimicking his mom's high-pitched, cheery voice.

"What a rip-off," Darcy said. "No one gives their customers something that's only half full."

"You just need to have a positive attitude," Mullet continued as he put his hands on his cheeks in mock happiness, "And think, wow, lucky me, my glass is half full today."

"I'm not coming back to this lemonade stand, ever, and I'm leaving you a bad review," Darcy said as she stalked off with her lemonade.

"Where the heck is she supposed to leave her review?" Mullet said.

"Who cares? She's gone and never coming back," Burt said and they both laughed and high-fived each other. They had managed to make money and get rid of Darcy in the same day. Nothing could be better.

—Chapter 4—
KID DETECTIVES

Burt banged his head on the table. "My life is falling apart."

While Darcy made good on her promise and they didn't see her again, they unfortunately didn't see much of anybody else either. A few of the neighbors bought some lemonade out of pity, but they had only managed to make a couple more dollars. It wasn't long before they were back in the dumps, realizing they were never going to get their Skyscrapers.

"There has to be a better way to make money," Burt said.

It was mid-afternoon on Sunday, and it was shaping up to be another hot and sticky day. They sold nothing when they opened after church until Burt's mom came out and bought a pity lemonade from each of them. She made things even worse when she gushed on and on about how it was the best lemonade she had ever had, and only took the hint that she was making them feel worse when Burt rolled his eyes.

"I better start laundry and check on your sister. Don't wear yourselves out too much today. You've got your first basketball practice tomorrow and you've got to be ready to go get them!" she said as she clapped her hands and bounced away.

Old Mr. Langley showed up right after that with only ten cents in his pocket. He seemed to think there was some sort of senior discount that increased with each day, and showed up with less money every time he came.

"Why do you keep letting him buy it for nothing?" Mullet finally asked.

"I can't help it. What if that's the last of his life savings?" Burt said, picking up the dime and scrutinizing it. "What if that was everything he had and now he can't afford food or his electric bill?"

"Oh, brother. You were not cut out to be a salesman, were you?" Mullet said as he flipped through his basketball cards for the hundredth time, one of the last remaining remnants of his father's existence. He looked up. "Maybe we could mow lawns."

"No one around here needs us to mow their lawns," Burt said.

"We could clean," Mullet said.

"I can't even keep my room clean," Burt moaned. His mother had already been on him about the state of his room. She said the smell was starting to frighten her. He explained to her that he was a businessman now, and he didn't have time to clean his room. Apparently, that wasn't the answer she was looking for, because she went on to inform him that he'd better get it clean by basketball practice… or he wasn't going.

"What's the groan for?" Mullet said as he pulled his eyes away from his card collection.

"My mom won't let me go to practice unless I get my room clean."

"Hey! That's what my mom said! They must have received some sort of mom group text reminding each other to bug us about our rooms. I don't know why it's so important to them. I mean it's not as if they have to live in there and…"

His sentence was cut short by a door slamming so loud that it shook the table.

Shoes clacked, echoing across the neighborhood. They both looked up to see the blur of Darcy Bell as she flew past them in a swish of pink and purple.

They looked at each other, eyes wide.

"Did it sound like she was crying to you?" Burt said.

Mullet shrugged. "I could only hear her stupid shoes clicking, besides, what's it to us if Darcy is crying? Whoever did it deserves a prize."

Burt couldn't argue with Mullet's logic, but on the other hand, he had never seen Darcy cry... ever. At school, she looked like she was nice in her dresses and bows, but she was downright tough and unlikeable. She was great at making other girls cry, but never cried herself. He looked back towards the bike trail that curved around Mullet's house and to the park, but she was long gone.

They went back to looking at Mullet's ancient set of basketball cards, still pristine in their plastic card holders. These cards had been looked over a million times, but Burt knew they made Mullet feel connected to his dad. Mullet had every card memorized and every stat secured in his head. If basketball card trivia existed, Mullet would be the king.

A throat cleared, which startled them as they both looked up. Darcy was standing next to their sign.

"How did she sneak up on us in those clicky shoes?" Mullet whispered.

Red blotches covered her face and her eyes were puffy. They both averted their eyes as she took a step closer.

"What's she doing coming down your driveway?" Mullet mumbled under his breath, "She promised she would never come back."

"Keep looking at the basketball cards, maybe if we don't make eye contact, she'll walk away."

They both stared down but knew their plan wasn't working when a quarter clinked into their empty jar.

"I'd like a full glass this time," she said with a scowl.

"One full glass of lemonade coming right up," Mullet said as he poured so much lemonade into the cup that it almost spilled over the top.

She grabbed it, sloshing some of it on the front of her dress as she drank the entire thing. She set her cup on the table and dug around in her wristband for another quarter. Out came a nickel and a few pennies, but nothing else.

"You can have a second glass for free," Burt said, cringing when he heard the words come out of his mouth. What was he thinking? He wasn't sure why he said it, and now the words had slipped out before he could stop, it was too late to change them now.

Mullet shot him a murderous look.

Crazily enough, Darcy didn't say anything. Not knowing what else to do, Burt poured more lemonade into her cup. He could feel Mullet's eyes boring into him and felt the heat increasing in his cheeks by the second. Burt didn't glance over as he slid the cup across the table to Darcy. This time, she sipped it slowly as she turned and watched her house.

"I'd give up my entire summer allowance if someone could get me out of the trouble I'm in," she said. Her shoulders started to shake, but at least she didn't start crying again.

Burt perked at the word allowance and leaned forward, "Really? I, uh mean, I'm sorry. Is there something we can do to help you? We have a lot of talents."

Mullet's face grew even redder, but Burt elbowed him in the ribs, hoping he would play along. This could be their chance.

For a moment Darcy turned away from them and Burt could see that she was wiping her eyes. By the time she turned back, she had shaken off the tears. Pretty impressive for a girl. "If you could actually help me, it would be worth every penny of my allowance."

The tension of Mullet's face slackened and he turned to Burt with wide eyes. Suddenly he was ready to hear what Darcy Bell had to say. "Go on."

"Someone ate my mom's really expensive peanut butter. She special orders this super fancy stuff online with chocolate and cherries and gold flakes. No one else is allowed to touch it. It's like her secret chocolate stash, except it is gourmet peanut butter instead. She just got two new jars in the mail and when she opened them this morning, they were empty!"

Darcy looked at the ground and kicked a small pebble across the driveway. Mullet looked at Burt and raised his eyebrows.

"Anyways, she thinks I'm the one who ate it," Darcy said as she crushed the lemonade cup between her hands and tossed it on the table. "I told her I didn't, but she's convinced I'm lying to her because I've taken her stuff before! Now she's grounded me until I tell her the truth! I'm not grounded for eating the peanut butter, but because she thinks I'm lying to her. I don't know how to convince her that I'm innocent. I am going to miss all my dance lessons, painting classes, and tryouts for the summer theater program. If I can't prove to her I'm not the one who stole her peanut butter, I won't be able to do anything." Darcy brought her palms to her eyes and barely managed to get her last few words out. "Everything is ruined."

"That sounds terrible," Burt said, trying to hide a snort, but by the look on Darcy's face, he didn't hide it well enough.

She glared at him. "How would you feel if you couldn't play basketball all summer? Huh? How would you feel then, Burt Lawrence?"

He gulped. Her voice was starting to scare him. "I'd feel like, like I couldn't face the day."

"Oh, I see, but somehow it's funny to you if it happens to me," she said, raising her eyebrows.

Suddenly Burt smiled at her with his biggest, most charming smile, and held out his hand.

She looked at it. "What are you doing? And what are you smiling about? Do you think it's funny that my entire life is destroyed?"

When Burt only smiled wider, she glared at Mullet, like somehow it was his fault. "What's your friend's problem?"

"Uh," he shrugged and looked at Burt.

"I would like to introduce myself," Burt said as he leaned forward and shook Darcy's hand. His large arm looked like an elephant leg as he tossed her scrawny one around, but he kept on shaking while he talked a million miles a minute. "I'm Burt, official kid detective and this here is my partner, Mullet. We're the local who-done-its of the neighborhood and we can solve any case, big or small." He just hoped he was just charming enough to pull off the idea brewing in his head.

She managed to yank her hand away from him and wipe it on her dress. She pulled hand sanitizer out of her wrist pouch and squirted it all over her palms, rubbing them vigorously. Then she took a few steps back and stared at them.

Burt looked down. Why did he always have to come up with crazy ideas? Now they looked dumb, and if she told anyone, it would give the silver spoons one more thing to harass them for. Nothing could get worse than being made fun of for playing pretend, and now she could have a heyday with it, bringing absolute ruin to their sixth-grade year. It would be their first year in middle school and now it was doomed before they even started.

He waited, but a snotty retort never came. In fact, Darcy looked relieved.

"You're detectives?" Darcy finally managed to say, looking between them with questioning eyes.

Trying to hide his surprise, he nodded and couldn't believe that she was actually falling for it.

"And you guys would help me with this case?"

They both nodded.

She folded her arms across her chest, looking more like her usual self. "Do you have any training? Because if you do, I'd pay just about anything to get my summer back in time to try out for the summer play and go back to my dance lessons."

"Really? Anything?" Mullet said a little too excitedly.

Burt kicked him beneath the table.

Mullet attempted a charming smile and wrapped his arm around Burt. "Burt here has his very own detective kit that we've used countless times. And you are in luck because we've just been sitting around, waiting for our next big case. The lemonade stand is actually our cover."

Burt held back a laugh. They hadn't even opened the detective manual, let alone solved a case. He had received the detective kit several months ago from his aunt and uncle for his twelfth birthday. The only thing they'd used was the magnifying glass to see if they could really fry worms on his driveway. But none of that mattered now, because the look on Darcy's face said that she was completely suckered in by their fake story.

"How long to solve a case?" she said.

"Two weeks," Mullet said.

"Two weeks?" She said as she drummed her fingers on the table.

"Two weeks," Mullet said confidently.

"So, if you solve the case in two weeks, I will give you my summer allowance." She paused for a second and then nodded. "Yeah, I would do that."

"And," Burt added quickly, "If we don't solve the case in two weeks, then you don't have to pay us anything. It's our guaranteed customer satisfaction guarantee."

Mullet leaned sideways and looked at him quizzically. "That's a lot of guarantee."

"Shh," Burt whispered under his breath, "Surely there's some statistic you can look up about guarantees, I think they always help the business."

"Okay, I'm in," she said, "But I'm not supposed to get any of my allowance because I'm grounded. If you prove that I'm innocent, my mom will owe me big time, and it's all yours if you solve it and get me my summer back."

"Good, then we will draw up an official detective contract and we'll all sign it after we discuss the details of the case."

Burt was impressed with how professional Mullet sounded. Normally he couldn't think quickly on the spot, or he would say something that got them into all kinds of trouble, but he actually sounded like a real detective. If Burt didn't know better, he would have thought that they had a real detective business too.

"Fine, where can I meet you to discuss the details?" she said as she looked around and lowered her voice, "It has to be somewhere private... and sometime after dark."

"Really?! A secret meeting after dark?" Mullet said, his eyes lighting up. He cleared his throat. "I mean, that's what we always do, right Burt? Undercover in the dark is the best time for detective work," he said, sounding professional again.

"Good, because I'm technically not allowed to leave the house right now."

They made plans to meet behind the tree in Burt's backyard at ten o'clock that night. She shook their hands, looking the happiest Burt had ever seen her as she hurried back to her house.

—Chapter 5—
BASKETBALL AND SECRET MEETINGS

That afternoon Burt and Mullet spent hours digging through piles of dirty laundry, candy wrappers, and sports equipment, trying to find the detective kit.

"Can I have your candy wrappers for my candy wrapper collection?" Mullet asked.

"Go for it," Burt said.

Anything that made his room look cleaner was better for him. Mullet got distracted looking through the various candy wrappers and adding them in alphabetical order to the other ones in his pocket.

Burt continued the search for the detective kit. Piles of dirty basketball clothes stood like mountains in the corner of his room, and he finally wrangled them into the laundry basket hoping to find his detective kit somewhere underneath. It wasn't on the floor, so he started pulling things out from under the bed. He finally located it under the back corner of his bed, smashed and slightly damaged, with a rotten apple core stuck to the lid. Luckily, everything inside still looked like new.

At the top of the box sat a book called, "The Detective's Guide to Being a Great Detective" in a plastic sleeve. Burt grabbed it and tossed it to the side to see what else was in the kit, but Mullet picked it back up.

"You know we should read this, right?"

"We don't need that, we'll use our intuition," Burt said, tapping his brain.

"No, we should read this cover to cover, so we know what to do. We have to do this detective thing by the book. We need all the facts."

That didn't surprise Burt at all. Mullet was a reader and a by-the-book kind of guy, who reveled in facts. He'd probably have fun reading the entire thing cover to cover. But to Burt, detective work seemed like a piece of cake. All they had to do was be observant and sneaky. Sneaky was their middle name. Even right now they were pulling off complete sneakiness. They might look like they were hanging out cleaning his room, but they were really getting ready for an undercover meeting. As for being observant, Burt figured they could be observant if they wanted to be observant. You just had to watch things. How hard could that be?

"See, listen to this. There's a list here of everything we need to be successful detectives and at the top of the list are things like a detective backpack to carry our things in and a detective notebook to track our cases. Neat, huh?" Mullet said as he stared intently at the pages and started making a list.

The first thing they decided to look for was a detective notebook. Burt knew just the place to find one. They sneaked into his sister's room and dug through the diaries hidden in the back of her closet.

"Score!" Burt said as he pulled one out and held it out for Mullet. On the cover his sister Jenna had written, "Keep Out or DIE" in silver letters. It was perfect to keep people from snooping through their cases, plus it had a lock. There were plenty of diaries left, so he figured she wouldn't notice if just one of them was missing. Another point for being sneaky.

He opened it up.

"Wait!" Mullet shouted, holding up his hands. "Maybe we shouldn't open that. I mean that's your sister's diary and my mom said it's not appropriate to read other people's personal stuff."

Ignoring him, Burt read, "Jenna's secret diary, DO NOT READ OR ELSE!" He tilted the diary towards Mullet, showing him where Jenna had drawn a dagger in silver pen. Red paint was splattered across the page like blood and the effect of everything looked so real, that Burt was almost afraid he would cut his finger on it if he touched it.

"Cool," Mullet said, as he sat beside Burt and ran his finger across the dagger. "I didn't know your sister was this awesome."

"I hope she doesn't pop out from somewhere and murder us," Burt said, looking around. "If she found us in here reading her diary, we'd be dead for sure."

"What's on the next page?" Mullet said, grabbing the diary. Mullet must have forgotten he was worried about her privacy as he turned to the page. "Oh!" he cried, heaving it across the room.

"What? Did she commit a crime? What's in there?" Burt said as he ran across the room and scooped up her diary. He opened it, expecting to find blood or something else equally awesome, but instead found a throng of bright red hearts scribbled all over the page.

"We'll have to tear that page out," Mullet said as he leaned over and ripped out the page, crinkled it into a ball, and made a perfect basket in the trash. He looked at the second page and jerked away from it. "Sick! Your sister likes Mackey Jones? Forget anything I said about your sister being cool. She was alright until I saw this. Now I am just creeped out."

"Give me that," Burt said as he reached for the diary and read the next page out loud. "Dear Diary,

Mackey Jones is the CUTEST boy in the ninth grade. Staring into his brown eyes is like staring into the soul of heaven. Barfaroni." He crumpled it up and shoved it in his pocket. "I can't read anymore or I'll gag."

"What's wrong with her? Geez, the next page has to go too," Mullet said, pointing to the words, "Mrs. Mackey Jones" surrounded by smudged pink lips. "She didn't actually kiss this, did she?" he said, dropping the book.

"We'll sanitize it," Burt said as they ripped out several more pages filled with thick red hearts and "Mrs. Mackey Jones" doodled in cursive all over them. Burt collected the pages and shoved them in his pocket. He would hide them under his bed later and hoped it was the one place his sister would never dare to venture. "Maybe I'll save those for someday when she threatens me."

Meanwhile, Mullet found a black marker and scrawled the word "CASES" in big bold letters right below the word "DIE", and bent the cover a little to make sure it looked used. More points for being sneaky. They were on a roll.

The next thing on the list was a backpack, which they found in a junk closet in the hallway. Burt was pretty sure it was his dad's from something and it was perfect because it was black.

"This is awesome," Mullet said as he tried it on.

"It's a little big," Burt said, noticing that the straps were falling off Mullet's thin shoulders. He grabbed the ends and pulled them tight, which made it fit better on Mullet's back, but left two straps dangling like long tails at the bottom.

"That feels better, besides we need something to hold all of our detective gear and this is black with a lot of pockets."

They stuffed their official detective backpack with two flashlights, a handful of old pencils, the worm-destroying magnifying glass, a fingerprint kit, and hats for disguises. They were feeling pretty professional by the time they headed to the tree for their meeting.

Burt and Mullet stood near the old oak tree in Burt's backyard, passing a frisbee to each other. They managed to convince Mullet's mom to let him spend the night for the second night in a row, under the condition that Burt would stay at their house the next night so that she could actually see her son. It was a good thing that they were next door neighbors. Their moms didn't mind if they ran back and forth between each other's houses, as long as they checked in every so often and kept their screen time to a minimum. It was another mom rule they lived by, but it was survivable if they had the run of the town every summer.

Burt's parents were sitting on the front porch, lost in conversation, and his older sister was gone for the night. He was pretty sure no one would notice them meeting with Darcy in the backyard. That was one thing they had decided on, no one could EVER know they were working with Darcy Bell.

First, she was a girl. Second, she ran with the silver spoons. They had always made sure to have nothing to do with her. But now that her family had moved to this side of town, would she still be allowed in that group or would she be considered an outcast too?

The frisbee whizzed by, and Burt heard a crack behind him. He turned around and saw Darcy slipping through the bushes. She was wearing black leggings and a dark green hoodie with the hood pulled way down over her forehead.

"Hey, we need to remember that for our disguises, I can barely see her in the dark," Burt whispered to Mullet as he casually tossed the frisbee in the brush. They pretended like they were trying to find it so they could sneak into the trees.

"Here, give me the notebook and I'll write it down. I'll look official if I'm writing something anyways," Mullet said as he stepped behind Burt and unzipped the backpack, pulling out the notebook and pens.

Darcy wiggled her way through the last of the bushes, glanced around, and made a run for the oak tree.

"I don't have much time, so let's hurry," she whispered.

"Um, okay," Burt said. He didn't know what to say and looked at Mullet for help, but Mullet was too busy scribbling in the notebook to notice. He looked back at Darcy, who was tapping her foot.

"Uh, first off, do you mind if we take notes?" Burt said trying to sound professional.

"I don't care what you do, let's just get this figured out so I can get my life back," Darcy said.

"Yes, well note taking is very important because notes help us remember the notes that you give us… uh, for our notes," Burt said.

"Noted," Darcy said with an eye roll as she folded her arms. She glanced at Mullet, probably hoping that he would talk instead. The silence continued and she started tapping her foot again.

"Did I miss something?" Mullet said, looking up from the notebook.

"I need to figure out our plan, and then I need to get home before my mom finds out I'm missing and grounds me for the rest of my life," Darcy huffed.

"It's like we agreed on earlier. We will work on your case for two weeks, and if we solve the crime, you give us your summer allowance. If not, you don't owe us anything for our time and skills," Mullet said.

"You know, I started thinking about it and that's a lot of money," Darcy said.

"Well, either we get paid for our detective work or you can kiss your theatre try-outs goodbye," Mullet said, sounding ruthless,

Darcy bit her lip. She didn't say anything as she glanced back toward her house. "Listen, you guys have done this before, right?" Darcy said.

"Loads," Mullet said, pointing to the backpack and waving Jenna's diary through the air. "Don't you see our used notebook and our official detective kit?"

"Okay, I mean, like how many cases have you solved?" Darcy said.

"We've solved every case we've had so far," Burt said, grinning at Mullet.

Burt noticed that Mullet was writing in the middle of the notebook, which was actually pretty smart now that he thought about it. It made it look like they had a notebook full of cases. Darcy leaned forward to look and Mullet snapped the notebook shut.

"Oh no you don't," he said, pointing his pencil at her, "These cases are top secret and we never expose our clients. We're confidential detectives."

"Oh," Darcy said, "Okay, well, that's good. I don't want anyone to know that..."

She stopped, but Burt could already guess at what she was going to say. She didn't want anyone to know that she had teamed up with them.

"If it helps, we don't want to be seen with you either," Burt said.

"If anyone saw us hanging out with you, that would be the end of us," Mullet said.

Darcy frowned at them but didn't say anything else about it. "Listen, I'll agree to the allowance thing if you solve this for me," she said, changing the subject, "But otherwise you get nothing... right?"

"Exactly, if we don't solve it, you get to keep your money," Mullet said.

"Money that I wouldn't get anyway because I'd still be grounded," she said glumly, "How am I supposed to talk to you? Not only do I not want to be seen with you, but my mom can't find me sneaking out. I'm supposed to be grounded and this is too far away for me to sneak away to."

"We need a secret headquarters," Mullet said.

"Yeah," Burt said.

"You're detectives and you don't have one?" Darcy said.

"We've never had a case that called for such special circumstances," Mullet said, tapping his pencil against his diary.

Burt nodded in agreement. At least Mullet had come up with something good to say.

"So, where are we going to meet?" Darcy said, starting to get impatient. She kept glancing back to her house and Burt knew she was probably worried her mom would completely freak if she found out that Darcy wasn't in her room.

Mullet had a blank look on his face, so Burt started thinking about all the places in the neighborhood. Neither of them had a tree house or a fort anywhere. He considered the park, but it was too far, especially if they had to meet at night. If his mom ever found out he was at the park after dark, he would never be allowed to leave again. It didn't seem like the other two could think of anything either. Finally, it hit him.

"What about the shed behind old man Langley's house?" Burt said.

Darcy frowned. "You mean that super nasty shed that's about to fall apart?"

"That's it," Burt said.

"It's perfect!" Mullet said.

"That's not how I would describe it," Darcy said as she scrunched her nose.

Burt continued. "But it is right next to your house, and no one would think to look there for anything... especially a secret detective agency. Old man Langley can barely get off his porch, so he probably doesn't use his shed, especially with all that tall grass."

"His stupid ugly grass is why my parents had to put up a privacy fence. His yard was making our yard look bad," she said, "But everything you're saying is true."

Burt grinned. He was really starting to like this whole detective scheme. It was pretty important to figure out where to have their secret headquarters.

"Okay, I'll just need you to sign here, and then we'll have a deal," Mullet said as he held out his pen and notebook to Darcy. The word "contract" was scribbled across the top of the page, with several sloppy sentences written below it.

Darcy took the notebook and squinted at it. "What's all that say?"

"That's just the fine print, no big deal. You just need to write in your information right there," he said as he pointed midway down the page where he wrote the words, "full name", "date", and "payment".

"So, this where I write what I'm paying you?" Darcy said.

"Yep," Mullet said.

"This better be worth it," she said with a sigh as she wrote on the page. She handed the notebook back to Mullet. "Yuck. There goes twenty dollars," Darcy said.

Burt's eyes bulged as he interrupted her. "You get twenty dollars for the summer?"

"No, I get twenty dollars every week, which you would already know if you hadn't interrupted me," Darcy said.

Mullet eyed Burt and Burt attempted to regain his composure. The kids they hung out with at school were lucky if they got a couple bucks a week, let alone twenty. No wonder the silver spoons on the team had the best of everything.

Darcy turned to leave, but Mullet stopped her. "We need to meet again to discuss the case!"

She looked at her house. "Listen, I've got to get back, like, right now. What time? Hurry!"

Mullet looked at Burt, who didn't skip a beat. "Tomorrow, same time, the shed," Burt said before she turned and ran back home.

Once they were in Burt's room, Mullet lost it. He whooped and jumped up and down. "I did the math. Twenty dollars for six weeks comes to one hundred and sixty dollars! We'll be rich!"

Between Darcy's allowance and the lemonade stand, they might actually be able to buy shoes by the summer tournament.

"Now all we need to do is get more business," Mullet said, rubbing his hands together.

"One crime at a time," Burt said, grinning, "One crime at a time."

—Chapter 6—
THE CLUBHOUSE

The next morning, Burt stood next to Mullet gazing at the shed.

"It looked better in my head," Burt said.

"Mine too…" Mullet said as they stared quietly.

The entire structure leaned heavily to the left and the door hung haphazardly on one hinge. There was also an undeniably stinky smell, one they couldn't place, making its way toward them.

"You know what? No. We were right. This is the perfect hideout for our secret headquarters. There's no way we're going to let Darcy tell us that it's not good enough. We'll make it the best detective headquarters that ever existed," Burt said.

"Yeah, and I'll get a construction book from the library," Mullet said.

The breeze picked up, carrying the wretched smell in their direction and the shed swayed, leaning even further to the left than before.

"What first?" Mullet said.

"We might want to straighten the walls before the wind blows the whole thing down," Burt said.

Mullet set their detective backpack down and walked over to the shed, while Burt scanned the backyard, making sure Mr. Langley wasn't around.

"Why does his yard look like the wilderness? If something was hiding in the grass, we'd never see it coming," Burt said.

An old apple tree even more gnarled than old Langley himself rose above them. Even if old man Langley looked out his back window, he wouldn't be able to see what they were up to.

"Okay," Burt said placing his hands on the wall. Mullet stepped next to him and they pushed the shed upright. It seemed to be holding itself in place, so they took a step back.

"Look at that, almost like new," said Mullet.

A gust of wind blew, and with a loud creak and shudder, the shed fell back into its slanted position.

"Bummer," Mullet said.

Burt looked around and found an old pile of wood in the side of the yard. He grabbed a half rotten two by four and wedged it into the ground. He looked up at Mullet. "Alright, you push, and I'll use this to hold it up straight."

Mullet pushed on the wall as hard as he could with his small frame, and Burt heaved the large board between the ground and the shed. They both let go and the shed stayed upright.

They added a few more boards to keep it steady and looked at their newly straightened clubhouse with pride. "Alright," Mullet said as he gave Burt a high five.

"What now?" Burt said, circling around the shed. "Should we fix the door next?"

"Actually, I was thinking we would leave the door like it is," Mullet said.

"But it looks like it's about to fall off," Burt said.

"Exactly. This is our secret headquarters. It needs to look abandoned, especially if Mr. Langley wanders out into this jungle of his. A fixed door would be a dead giveaway," Mullet said.

"So, we have a secret door?" Burt said grinning.

"Yes," Mullet said, "Follow me." He walked around to the back of the shed. "Everyone has to come through the yard this way, so we'll just have them come through the back of the shed… through our secret door," he said, beaming proudly.

Burt walked up to the back wall and pushed on all of the boards. One, in particular, was pretty loose and swung easily to the side, giving them plenty of room to squeeze through.

"Dude, secret entrance," Burt said as he gave Mullet a thumbs up and shimmied between the boards. The moment he entered, his lungs inhaled something rancid. He recoiled, sputtering and coughing as he tried to get away. Mullet came in behind him, but Burt shoved him back. "Out! Out! Abort the mission! Abort the mission!" he said through heaving coughs.

Mullet backed out in a hurry, grabbing Burt and pulling him out through the boards. "What? What is it?"

He dropped on his hands and knees, trying not to vomit from the smell.

"What? What was it? Poison? Gas?

Finally, after taking several huge gulps of fresh air, Burt sat, shuddering. "It's something dead."

"Oh no, did something happen to old man Langley?"

"No, it's not him. I think it's a dead raccoon covered in maggots," Burt said. Just the thought of it made him want to hurl again.

"Cool!" Mullet said as he swung the board open and stuck his head inside. "Ugh, it reeks," he said as he tried to yank himself out. "Burt! Burt!"

"Yeah?"

"Hey, I'm stuck, get me out of here!"

Even though Mullet was small, the oversized backpack had gotten caught just right between the boards.

Burt managed to pull him out and they both stepped far away, trying to get a breather. "Yeah, I don't think Darcy is going to stick around if we make her go in there," Burt said.

"This has to be our headquarters, it's the best place," Mullet said. He unzipped their detective backpack and rummaged around until he found trash bags, swimming goggles, clothespins, and two pairs of bright yellow rubber gloves. He ripped a trash bag off the roll and tore a hole in the bottom of it.

"What are you doing that for?" Burt said, "Won't the raccoon fall out the bottom?"

"This isn't for the raccoon dummy," Mullet said as he pulled the trash bag over his head and tossed the second one at Burt. "Put it on. Time for maggot raccoon extraction."

Burt slipped it over his head, donning his trash bag outfit. They pulled on the rubber gloves and made sure their eyes and noses were sealed with the goggles and clothespins. They quickly made their way into the shed. Burt's stomach shuddered as the smell started to make its way to his nostrils. They scooped the raccoon into another trash bag and dragged it out of the shed.

"Now what?" Burt said.

"I didn't think that far ahead," Mullet said, gagging.

There was no way they could leave it anywhere in Langley's yard, and today was trash day, so it would be hard to get it in someone's trash can without being seen.

"My mom's at work. Maybe we should bring it to my yard and bury it or something," Mullet said.

It was the best idea that they could think of, so holding the bag loosely between each other, they made their way to Mullet's yard. In the far corner stood a patch of several evergreen trees, which looked like a decent place to bury an animal.

As they laid the trash bag on the ground, they heard someone call to them.

"Hey! Garbage boys!"

They turned around to find Mark, Peter, and Danny riding towards them on their bikes.

"Quick, toss it over there!" Mullet said as he stepped in front of Burt. Burt quickly flung the garbage bag somewhere behind him. He heard it land with a thud and turned around to face the silver spoons.

"What did you guys do, go swimming in the garbage pit today?" Peter said as he rode by, skidding to a stop.

"Or is that all your moms could afford for you to wear to the pool for the summer?" Mark taunted.

"Shut up!' Mullet yelled as they snickered and started to ride away. He started to chase after them, but

Burt caught the puffy part of his trash bag and pulled him back.

"You won't catch them," Burt said.

They looked at each other through their partially fogged goggles. "We're ruined," Mullet said as they stared at each other.

"Why are they going to this park anyways?" said Burt, "Don't they have that fancy country club with the new courts that they're always bragging about?"

"And the pool," Mullet said.

"And the golf course," Burt added. He doubted any of them even played golf, but it didn't stop them from always bringing up the country club they all belonged to, including the golf carts they were allowed to drive anywhere they wanted.

"Let's go," Mullet said as he turned.

Suddenly they heard a thud and a bunch of shouting. They crept into the pine trees to find that Burt had accidentally chucked the trash bag onto the park path. Peter had hit it with his bike and kicked up the remains of the raccoon on Mark and Danny.

"We better get out of here before they think we did that on purpose," Burt said as he and Mullet ran as fast as they could back to the shed.

Without the raccoon inside, the shed didn't seem so bad anymore. The inside was littered with old trash and cobwebs, but with a little work, it cleaned up well. They rolled logs into the shed and laid a few old boards over two of them to make a desk and added a few more for chairs. They hung up garden tools that looked older than Mr. Langley, which was hard to believe. Nothing looked older than him. They righted shelves that had fallen down, nailed loose boards into place, and brushed off a potting bench to hold their detective supplies. The bench had several eyehooks screwed into it, and Mullet was suddenly thrilled to figure out which of their supplies he could hang where.

He hung their backpack on the largest one, and their magnifying glass and flashlights on three smaller ones. He dug a rusty tin can out of the trash bag and filled it with stubby pencils and some sparkly gel pens they had also stolen from Burt's sister, Jenna. Finally, they stepped back, gazing proudly at their display of detective supplies.

Running back to Burt's house, they found his mom had already set out food for lunch. After the whole raccoon incident, Burt didn't think he would ever be able to eat again, but his stomach rumbled at the sight of food.

His mom stood in the kitchen pulling lunchmeat and cheese out of the fridge. Baked beans steamed on the stove beside mac and cheese. The counter was covered with buns, pickles, and bags of chips. After all that work, they were starving and piled their plates high with food.

Burt's mom murmured something about growing boys when everything she laid out instantly disappeared, but he knew she secretly loved it when they ate all her food.

After they finished, they set up their lemonade stand to keep their cover. Mullet set out homemade detective business cards for the neighborhood kids to take.

Tiana, who was two years younger than them, walked down from her house at the end of the block. She handed them her quarter, but didn't reach out to grab her lemonade when Burt handed it to her. She was staring at the business cards.

"You're real detectives?" she said, looking up at them.

"Yep, we're official," Burt said as he tapped the rectangular card on the table. He'd thought of the idea of making them detective cards on the back of some of his mom's old business cards from when she sold artwork.

Burt handed the card to her and could only hope that she didn't think to turn the card over. That wouldn't look official with its flowered border and girly script.

"I need a detective," she said, "I'm missing a very important bracelet. Do you think you could find it? I have two dollars that I could give you to find it." She reached into a sparkly green wristband on her arm and pulled out two crinkled dollar bills. Her big brown eyes looked so hopeful when she held them out, that Burt already knew he was caving.

Mullet and Burt looked at each other and said "yes" in unison. Mullet wrote out another contract, took the information on the bracelet, and had her sign it.

Burt explained they would return the two dollars if they didn't find her bracelet in two weeks.

"We're like a real infomercial, money-back guarantee if the customer isn't totally satisfied," Mullet said, beaming with pride. He nudged Burt and whispered under his breath, "I did look it up and customer satisfaction guarantees are bogus, but I definitely think we can solve any crime."

Burt still wasn't convinced that they could really do it. They had less than two weeks to solve two crimes, and they had never done any detective work before in their lives.

—Chapter 7—
THE GAME PLAN

The detective work was a distraction from the nervousness of their first basketball practice, but now that it was here, they couldn't ignore it any longer. It was time to face their teammates, who happened to be the people they tried to avoid the most during the school year.

While they were unloading their sports bags from the car, Burt could have sworn he felt something land on his shoulder. He turned, but didn't see anything.

It happened again as they were walking to the courts, but this time something landed and stuck to his leg. He reached down and pulled out some sort of candy wrapper lined with something gooey. He looked up and caught a glance of someone behind the athletic shed.

"Mullet, can you see who's over there?" Burt said.

They watched as a hand reached into the trash can, grabbed something out, and threw it in their direction.

Mullet stomped over there. "What's the big idea?"

Peter stepped out and grinned. "Where's your trashy uniform and goggles? Leave it at home?"

Mullet balled his hand into a fist, but Burt pulled him away. Other than the fact that Peter would pound him, they weren't allowed to fight. Coach Clay said any fighting would get them kicked off the team.

Coach Clay made it pretty obvious he favored the silver spoons. His motivational talk consisted of him using Peter and Mark as examples and he beamed at them constantly, like they were his Olympic medals or something.

When the torture finally ended, he sent them on the half-mile lap around the community walking path. It was a three-quarter mile loop around the outside of the park. Running wasn't Burt's favorite thing, but he was more than happy to get off the bench and focus on something besides the snickers of Peter and his gang. The rest of the team sprinted off without them as they hung back and took a few drinks from their water bottles.

The coach's whistle blew. "Burt! Mullet! Get a move on. If you're going to be on this team, then you can't stand around being lazy!"

There was no explaining to him that they were avoiding their stuck-up teammates, so they took off. Other than trying to avoid moms pushing strollers and old couples on their evening walks, jogging felt good. As they rounded the turn by the community gardens, Peter jumped out from behind a tree.

"Boo! You don't belong on this team, you're nothing but trash," he said, flicking a nasty pop bottle at them.

"Go back to your mommy's free day camp at the library," Mark joined in, tossing more trash in their direction.

Burt looked at Mullet, who was trying desperately to keep his calm, but looked ready to launch himself at them at any second. He might be small, but his anger was big and could blow to the size of Mount Everest in an instant if Burt didn't do something quick.

"Mullet, calm down. We can't lose our spot on the team. Let's push it," Burt whispered under his breath.

Unlike the silver spoons, they were used to walking, or better yet, running everywhere on their side of town. They raced from the park, to the library, to the sandwich shop, and to Ben's family-owned grocery store, where their mothers sent them on last-minute errands.

It was nothing to leave the others in the dust as they picked up their pace and sprinted the rest of the way around the walking path.

Coach Clay raised his eyebrows as they hustled onto the court, beating their teammates by a long shot. The most satisfying part was when the rest of the team trickled in behind them, huffing and puffing as they fell on the ground in agony.

"Get some water," Coach Clay said as he jotted notes on his clipboard.

At the benches, the other boys started whispering taunts under their breaths.

"Hey trash boys, running fast won't keep you from sitting the bench this summer," Peter said.

"Hey! What's going on over there?" the coach yelled.

Peter grinned, not missing the beat. "Nothing coach, just talking some trash with the team!" he said as he thumped Burt on the back, causing the rest of the team to snigger.

"A little friendly competition is always good. Everyone to the center of the court," he said as he turned back around. He studied his clipboard and started running them through drills.

The drills were difficult, which was a relief to Burt and Mullet because the other guys were too tired to pick on them anymore.

When they jumped into the van, Mrs. Mullet asked them at least thirty times why they were so quiet on the way home. They replied thirty times that they were just tired, but Burt could tell that she didn't believe them. Thankfully she stopped asking.

Neither of them felt like telling her, or anyone else for that matter, that they were getting bullied. Their only hope was their new detective agency and earning enough money for the shoes that would make everything right. Once they had the shoes, Peter and the other guys wouldn't be able to say anything anymore. The shoes would fix all of their problems.

They helped Mullet's mom unload groceries when they got back. "You still like quesadillas, don't you Burt?" she said.

"They're still my favorite," he said. Somehow food made him forget about the awful practice.

"Dinner won't be long," she said as she started opening jars of salsa and shredding cheese.

After they ate, they played a round of cards with her. Mullet asked if they could go outside.

When she said yes, they made a beeline for the door as she yelled, "Don't be out past dark!"

"Got it, Mom!" Mullet yelled over his shoulder as they hurried to their brand-new secret meeting place.

To their surprise, Darcy was already waiting for them.

"You're late," she said.

Mullet looked at his watch and looked back at her. "By one minute."

"Still, that's one minute of my time wasted and I have to make this fast before my mom decides to make a surprise prison round and figures out that I'm not in the house," Darcy said.

She was sitting on one of the logs behind their makeshift desk, which meant that only one of them could sit. Mullet had the notebook, so Burt told him to take it and stood uncomfortably beside him.

"So, what do you need to know?" Darcy said.

"Why don't you tell us the story from the beginning," Mullet said. He put the tip of his pen to the paper and looked up at her.

She folded her arms and leaned back against the wall.

"Well, about a week ago my mom received a package of her favorite peanut butter. It's gourmet," Darcy said with a dramatic pause. "That means it's really expensive."

"We know that," Mullet said.

"Right," Darcy said like she didn't believe him, "Anyways, my brother and I really like peanut butter, so she bought some cheaper peanut butter for us. I mean not cheaper like the cheap stuff that you guys probably eat, but cheaper like it wasn't as expensive as hers. Anyways, she told us not to touch her mail-order peanut butter or else. When she went to eat it, it was gone."

"The jar or the peanut butter?" Mullet said.

"The peanut butter. The jar was still there with some peanut butter smeared on the sides, but there wasn't even enough for a spoonful. She screamed for me to come downstairs and accused me of eating it. I told her I didn't eat any peanut butter from any of the jars yet, but she didn't believe me. She grounded me until I decide to tell her the truth and now I can't do anything or go anywhere until I confess. I'm a prisoner in my own house."

"She didn't talk to your brother?" Mullet said.

Darcy sighed. "That's the problem, he left for camp this week, so he couldn't have touched the second jar."

"So, we can rule your brother and your mom out," Mullet said. He tapped the pen against his temple. "Who else has been in and out of your house over the last few weeks?"

"Well, lots of people," Darcy said, "My dad, my aunt, the gardener, the cleaner, my babysitter, my grandma... my mom's friends. We have a really nice house, so people like to hang out there."

Burt tried not to gag at how snotty she sounded.

Mullet was still writing, so Burt tried to think of something to say. "Which people were around when the peanut butter disappeared?"

Darcy scrunched her nose as she thought about it.

"I don't know. It's hard to say. I guess everyone has been around, except for my grandma and my dad. The babysitter is here every day, and the housekeeper and gardener are here a few days a week."

Mullet circled the babysitter and then put check marks next to the gardener and the cleaner.

"Anything else?" Darcy said.

"That should do it," Mullet said as he snapped the notebook closed. "My colleague and I will discuss the case and I suggest we meet back here tomorrow to go over our plan to solve it. Same time?"

"Can we meet later, like after my parents are in bed?" Darcy said.

Burt nodded and she looked relieved.

"Okay, tomorrow, eleven o'clock," Darcy said as she flew out the door.

Burt sat down and looked at Mullet. "What do you think?"

"I think we need to look at the babysitter first. If she's there all the time, she might get hungry and eat the peanut butter when no one is watching."

"She sounds like our best bet. Do you think the gardener even goes inside at all? If not, he can probably be ruled out as the culprit."

"Oh right," Mullet said. He wrote a little note next to the gardener and stared at the rest of the paper.

"Enough of this detective stuff," Burt said, "Right now we need to think about what we're going to do about basketball practice tomorrow night."

—Chapter 8—
THE PLAN

If their first practice was bad, the second one was worse. None of the guys could stop talking about how their parents pre-ordered the SkyScraper Pros. They would all have them in their mailboxes by Friday and for practice the following Monday. That is, everyone but Burt and Mullet. The worst part was that now that they had made it through practice, they had to go home and meet with Darcy. It wasn't their idea of a perfect day.

Eleven o'clock hit and Darcy still wasn't in the headquarters. Five minutes ticked by, then ten, then fifteen and she still wasn't there. They were about to leave when they heard hurried footsteps approaching.

"Hello?" Darcy called as she ran around the shed and swung open the door. It smacked Burt across the back of the head as she whipped it open, and he lost his balance, toppling off the log he was using as a chair.

"Geez," he said, rubbing the spot that was starting to swell, "Be careful! You're not even supposed to be using that door. That's not our secret entrance and the screws are so loose that it will probably fall off."

"Your head or the door? I'm not sure which one is screwed on looser," she said.

The temperature of the shack seemed to rise several degrees as he fumed. Normally Burt was calm and collected, but Darcy had a way of pushing him over the edge. Thankfully, Mullet nodded towards the poster of the SkyScraper Pros on the wall, and Burt forced himself to settle down.

"So," Mullet said, taking a break from his usual note-taking, "We have a plan to catch the peanut butter thief."

"You do? Is it any good?"

He stopped. "What do you think we are, amateur detectives? Burt, you tell her, it was your idea."

Burt didn't feel like helping Darcy now, especially with the splitting headache he was starting to get. Mullet tilted his head towards the picture of the SkyScrapers a second time.

"Why do you keep making those freaky head movements?" Darcy said.

"What head movements?" Mullet said, immediately straightening his head.

Darcy rolled her eyes. "Let's just get this over with. Tell me your great plan."

If they didn't need the shoes, Burt would just tell her to get lost, but he tried to forget his pounding head and attempted to use a nice voice as he spoke. "We thought we would make peanut butter cookies. Then you could hand them out to everyone at your house, while we hide and spy on them. If we can see who likes them best, or you know, who takes the most, then we can narrow down our list of suspects."

Darcy smiled. Burt realized that it was the first real smile that he had ever seen on her face. At school she never really seemed that happy at all.

"Okay, yeah, I like that plan," Darcy said, "When are we going to do it?"

"When will the most people be around?" Mullet said, "It would be nice if we could at least try and give a cookie to everyone on our list that could be a potential suspect."

Burt gave Mullet a thumbs up. Their detective language actually sounded convincing.

"Okay, well my brother gets home tomorrow evening. My babysitter will be here. The house cleaner will be here, and then my mom, aunt, grandma, and some other family are stopping in because they are all going out to eat. The only person we won't see is the gardener."

"Anytime tomorrow works for us because we don't have practice," Burt said.

"Good because you're running out of time," Darcy said, "So far we've only had these dumb meetings and you haven't done anything."

"Look up there," Mullet said, pointing to the "One Hundred Best Tips for Great Detectives" poster from the kit that he nailed to the wall. "Tip number one says that a great detective must always be prepared. We take that very seriously, so if you want the job done right, stop complaining."

Darcy narrowed her eyes at him and started to pack up her stuff.

Uh oh. Burt had to do something. Blocking the door with his body, he held up his hands. "What he was trying to say is that we are prepared for tomorrow and ready to put the plan into place to catch the thief."

They both seemed to settle down. Thank goodness. If they didn't get those shoes they could forget ever showing their faces on any basketball team ever again.

"It's settled," Burt continued, "We'll meet here tomorrow evening and get set up from there."

"Don't forget the cookies," Darcy said as she rushed out the door.

—Chapter 9—
THE COOKIES

"Wait, now do we add the eggs?" Mullet said as he squinted at the shabby recipe card.

Burt snatched it away from him and looked at it. They managed to convince his mom that they were going to sell peanut butter cookies at their lemonade stand, leaving out the part about using it to discover the peanut butter thief.

"Yeah, add the eggs. I don't think it really matters because it's all going into the same bowl, right?" Burt said.

"Sounds good to me," Mullet said.

They finished the cookies in time to open their lemonade stand again for the afternoon.

"Can't I eat one?" Mullet said as he opened the bag.

Burt pulled it away from him. "No way, we don't know how many we'll need, plus my mom needs to see us selling some at our lemonade stand. Remember, it's our cover," Burt said.

The lemonade stand was unsuccessful and they packed up early to get ready for their trap to capture the peanut butter thief.

A knock came on the door while they were packing their things, and Mullet's mom started to open it.

"Quick, hide that stuff," Mullet said as he cracked open the door.

Burt quickly tried to shove everything under the bed, but Mullet already had so much stuff shoved under there that nothing would fit. He chucked the diary behind Mullet's desk and sat on the backpack.

Mullet's mom stepped in and looked around. "You have got to get this room clean. Listen, I have to run back to the library to get some work done, so you two have fun and behave. Eat whatever you want."

"Okay," they said in unison.

"That was close," Mullet whispered as he got up to close the door.

"Why does it matter if she sees the detective's guide? It's not that big of a deal," Burt said.

"Because if you read 'The Detective Guide to Being a Great Detective,' or the DGB as I like to call it for short, it says that good detectives are elusive. If anyone sees our stuff, especially my mom, then it shows we're not elusive and we're not really good detectives. Plus, we're spying on the neighbors," Mullet said.

"Oh right," Burt said. His mom definitely wouldn't like that.

Four o'clock came and Mullet moved with sudden energy. "C'mon, hurry up! It's the perfect day to catch a thief."

Mullet went through the backpack and checked things off the list on his clipboard one more time.

"We already checked everything," Burt moaned.

"Don't knock it, Santa checks his list twice," Mullet replied, not bothering to look up from his clipboard.

"Good thing your mom said we could eat anything, I'm starving," Burt said as he opened the pantry. He pulled out a bag of tortilla chips and a jar of Mrs. Mullet's homemade salsa.

They went over their plans one more time as they ate the entire bag of chips.

From there, they left Mullet's house, crept through Burt's backyard, and made their way along the edges of the neighbor's yards, praying that no one would see them. They didn't anticipate the dog at Darcy's house and sat crouched behind a bush as the dog jumped and yelped, doing its best to let the entire neighborhood know they were there.

"We should have brought dog treats," Burt muttered.

"I'll add that to the list, but what are we going to do right now?" Mullet said.

"Back up! Hurry!"

"I can't," Mullet said, "The backpack got stuck on something."

Burt ran around him and found where the long strap of the backpack had snagged on a branch. He worked hard to pull it free and finally ripped it, as they stumbled back behind the privacy fence.

The dog appeared to be contained by some sort of invisible fence, but was jumping five feet into the air and shrieking with a high-pitched bark, alerting all the neighbors like an ambulance.

Suddenly it stopped and turned around, darting for the house. Darcy stepped around the corner shaking a bowl of dog food while yelling, "Here Griffin! Here, boy!"

As soon as she set the bowl down, the dog no longer cared that they were hiding in the bushes and busied himself gobbling up his food.

Darcy walked over to them. "Not so great, detectives. Aren't you supposed to be sneaky?" she whispered.

"Aren't you supposed to warn us about the dog?" Burt said back.

She stuck her tongue out at him.

"Stop," Mullet said, "We've got to follow through on our plan."

"This way," she said as she led them around the side of the house, talking as they followed her. "My dad is getting home with my brother in an hour and my mom should be back with my grandma about the same time. Everyone is supposed to meet up here and go out to eat."

She stopped outside the window. "This is my dad's study. The window is unlocked, so just climb in. I have chores to finish, so I'll get you later."

She took off and they were left standing by the window.

"One more thing," she said as she popped back around the corner, "Here's your warning, the babysitter is here, but she's not as bad as the dog."

"What's that supposed to mean?" Mullet whispered.

"Ignore it," Burt said as he figured out how to slide the window open. He put his hands together, so Mullet could step on them and get a boost up. Then he grabbed each side of the window and hoisted himself up with Mullet's help.

They shut the window and turned. Animals stared back at them from every corner of the room.

"They're watching us," Mullet whimpered as he inched away from a wild boar with long thick tusks and glassy black eyes.

"I'm beginning to wonder about Darcy's dad," Burt said as he pressed himself against the window next to Mullet. If the wild boar seemed bad, the full-sized grizzly bear directly across the room was even worse. It stood on its hind legs with its paws raised in the air like it was going to tear something apart. Sharp teeth glistened in its mouth, which was wide open in mid-roar. Right beside it was a full-sized crocodile displayed on a table with its mouth curved into a horrible grin.

"Let's stay right here," Mullet said as he slid down the wall and drew his knees to his chest. Burt agreed and they sat unmoving, waiting for Darcy to arrive.

Ten minutes later, the door swung open and Darcy stepped in. She took a minute to catch her breath and looked around, finally spotting them beneath the window.

"Why are you sitting over there? You could have sat on the couch or one of the chairs you know. It's not like my dad will know the difference," she said.

Mullet glanced at the boar and flinched. Good thing they were wearing disguises, or she would be able to see just how scared they were. Mullet couldn't get any words out, so Burt spoke up. "We didn't want to leave, um, our fingerprints on anything."

"Right, yeah, fingerprints…" Mullet said, still so bewitched by the animals that he could barely squeeze the words out.

"Oh," Darcy said as she sat on her dad's couch. "Well, I doubt he'll be scanning this place for fingerprints any time soon. It's not like he regularly checks this room, or for that matter, anywhere in the house for fingerprints. Anyways, just to let you know, my dad doesn't like peanut butter."

Neither of them budged.

She scrunched her face up. "Why are you still sitting like that? You should at least come over and talk with me."

They looked at each other and shuffled hesitantly across the room, trying not to make any eye contact with the animals. By the time they made it over to Darcy, Mullet literally leapt onto the couch, and dove behind the pillows.

"My babysitter is watching TV, but not really, because she's actually staring like a zombie at her phone. She's the worst babysitter ever, but probably the best if you're trying to be sneaky, so I can sneak you out of here as soon as my mom leaves to get my grandma. Then I'll give you a tour of the house. Oh! That's my mom! I better go."

As soon as the study door shut, the eyes of the wild animals seemed to bulge and their teeth seemed to grow even bigger.

"Mullet?" Burt said, "What do you think we should do?"

"Hide behind a pillow and don't move a muscle."

The minutes ticked by and Mullet lifted his head. "Burt"?

"Yeah?"

"When I grow up, I'm not getting a house with a study, even if it means I have to give up my mansion."

"Ditto," Burt replied.

The minutes ticked by slowly, and Burt wondered if Darcy was ever going to show up. Finally, they heard a quiet knock at the door and, without saying anything, she waved them over. Mullet flung himself from the couch and was out the door at lightning speed.

They tiptoed past the living room, but the sitter didn't pull her eyes from her phone, not even when Mullet tripped over his backpack strap and crashed on the hallway floor.

The rooms in Darcy's house were gigantic, with huge windows to let in lots of light. Everything in the house was gigantic, fancy, and expensive. The carpets were thick and soft, and the furniture was polished and shiny.

They ended up in Darcy's craft room, which was full of paints, paper, colored tapes, glue, pens, and pencils. Framed paintings of horses, butterflies, and sunsets hung on the walls.

"Cool artwork," Burt said as he stared at a picture of a butterfly that looked almost real.

"Thanks," Darcy said, sounding genuinely kind, "I painted it."

They were so good that Burt couldn't believe Darcy had actually painted them. It was hard to imagine the tough girl from school sitting at home painting things like butterflies and flowers. Not only that, but she was good at it. No wonder she didn't want to miss her art classes.

Darcy grabbed a book and flopped down in a fluffy black beanbag. "Help yourself to whatever," she said pointing to the other fuzzy beanbags scattered around the room.

Mullet eyed the beanbags and pointed at them.

"What is it?" Darcy said impatiently once she realized that neither of them were sitting down.

"Please tell me that your dad didn't shoot those too? They aren't some type of weird unicorn or yeti that's stuffed, are they?" Mullet said.

"Oh my gosh," she said, "Do you see eyes or a mouth? They aren't living creatures. They're beanbag chairs."

"They aren't alive now..." Burt said.

"They weren't alive ever!"

They sat down and finally got bored enough to look around. Mullet found a book about crazy world facts to read, and Burt started building a tower out of colored Popsicle sticks and paint bottles.

The clock dinged and Darcy stood up. "Listen, everyone should be here soon. I'll go downstairs and check everything out and then hide you in the dining room we don't normally use. Then you can watch people and take whatever notes you need while I hand out the cookies."

Mullet stood and strapped on his backpack. "Here we go, a real stakeout," he said as they followed Darcy down the enormous staircase.

She led them through the open halls, and into a huge dining room. The chairs were covered in emerald cloth and carved with fancy details. A long white tablecloth was draped across the table and she held it up so they could crawl underneath.

The babysitter was still in the living room, and Darcy walked to the kitchen to put the peanut butter cookies on a plate.

A few minutes later, the front door opened.

"Darcy darling," a cheerful voice sang out.

Suddenly a flood of people came through the door, chatting and talking and hanging their things up. The babysitter and house cleaner walked into the foyer to greet them. Darcy followed behind, carrying a fancy crystal tray piled high with peanut butter cookies.

"Did you make these Darcy my darling girl?"

"Yes, Grandma, I made them earlier. I thought it would be a nice way to welcome Hank back home, and everyone else too."

"How thoughtful," Darcy's mother said, "Did you clean up the kitchen?"

"Yes," Darcy said as everyone oohed and aahed over the cookies.

The cookies actually did look good and Burt felt proud of their baking abilities. He and Mullet watched as everyone took one, except for Darcy's aunt and dad. Good thing Mullet was furiously scribbling away, making sure not to miss any important observations. Before long, they would discover the thief and have all the money they needed for shoes. This was it.

Everyone put the cookies into their mouths.

Instantly their faces contorted into awful shapes as everyone started choking and coughing.

"Blech!" Darcy's brother spit his cookie into one hand and used the other to wipe his tongue.

"Wow, Darcy, these are, um," Darcy's grandma started, but couldn't finish as she choked and waved her hand in front of her reddening face.

The housekeeper grabbed a basket of cloth napkins, a pitcher of water, and several glasses. She quickly distributed them around the room.

"Disgusting," Hank said as he bolted into the kitchen and ran his mouth underneath the sink faucet.

Darcy's mother quickly apologized to everyone as Darcy stood there speechless, her face flaming neon red.

The commotion calmed down as everyone sipped their water and spit the cookies into the trash. They grabbed their things to head out for dinner, joking about needing to get the taste out of their mouths.

As soon as everyone was out the door, Darcy poked her head into the dining room. "I'm going to kill you for embarrassing me like that in front of my entire family. You can see yourselves out," she hissed and slammed the front door.

Once they heard the cars pull away, they climbed out from under the table. Burt grabbed a cookie from the tray and snapped it in two, handing half of it to Mullet. They stuffed the cookies in their mouths and made an immediate beeline for the kitchen.

"That was disgusting," Burt said as he gulped down more water.

It was time to get out of there, so they grabbed the bag of peanut butter cookies, hurried to the study, and climbed out the window. As soon as their feet hit the ground, Griffin charged around the corner and started barking like a maniac.

"Run for it!" Mullet yelled as he dropped from the window and booked it across the lawn.

"Nice doggy, nice Griffin," Burt tossed some of the cookies over his head. It was enough to get Griffin to stop chasing them for a moment, giving them the time they needed to jump over the fence.

They stopped to catch their breath and peek through the slats. Griffin gobbled up a cookie and started to hack and cough.

"That'll teach him to bark at us," Mullet said as Griffin ran to his water bowl and started lapping up water.

They ran to Burt's house and burst through the back door.

"Burt? Mullet? Is that you?" Burt's mom called from the kitchen.

"Yeah," Burt said.

"Did you try those cookies you made? Please tell me you didn't sell any because something went very wrong."

—Chapter 10—
THE GROCERY STORE

The next morning, they were hanging out in their headquarters when the door swung open, knocking Burt in the head a second time as Darcy burst through.

"That's not the right door!" Burt said as he jumped up. He was about to yell at Darcy, but Mullet beat him to it.

"Listen, this is OUR headquarters. It belongs to me and Burt and it's for OUR business. It's top secret, so you can't just barge in here anytime you want. What if we were working on a top-secret case?" Mullet said.

"Well, you better be working on a case... my case! The peanut butter cookie idea failed, and I spent the entire day getting made fun of. They even had the chef at the restaurant come out and share tips on making cookies with me. Everyone was laughing at me. Even my own grandma laughed at me! I should just fire you both now," she shouted.

"Okay, just calm down before old Langley hears you yelling," Burt said.

Darcy rolled her eyes. "That prehistoric dinosaur can't hear anything."

"With your loud voice, you could wake the dead," Mullet said.

She folded her arms and glared at them. Burt almost thought about telling her they were through, but the poster of the SkyScraper Pros gleamed behind her, so he bit his tongue. He regained his composure and decided to talk as calmly as he could. He knew if he figured out how to stay calm, Mullet would follow suit. He took a deep breath.

"Okay, we're detectives, so we always have a backup plan. We are going to go down to the grocery store and buy a jar of peanut butter. Then we are going to plant it in your cupboard and hideout to see who eats it. We know we can catch the peanut butter thief, it's just a matter of setting the right trap," Burt said.

"Okay, let's go right now," Darcy said.

"Now?" they both said in unison.

"My mom is having a big dinner party this weekend for my grandma, so the house cleaner will be back, along with the sitter, the gardener, and most of the family. It's our best chance."

"Dinner party?" Mullet said.

"Yeah, you know, people come over to eat a fancy meal," Darcy said.

Burt hit Mullet's shoulder, "Like when we have friends over for pizza."

"I said fancy, like an actual fancy meal."

"Okay," Burt said, "So when we buy expensive pizza."

"Never mind," Darcy said as she rolled her eyes.

If she kept rolling her eyes, Burt was convinced that they would get stuck like that someday. Then only the whites of her eyes would show, and she wouldn't have any eyeballs anymore. He couldn't decide if that would make her look more or less creepy than she already did. He'd have to tell Mullet his theory later.

"You guys aren't very refined, are you?"

"We're refined when it comes to basketball," Burt offered.

"Never mind, let's just get to Ben's grocery store before it closes."

Burt told his mom they were heading to the park. It wasn't a complete lie, because if they took the long way around the park, they would still end up at Ben Hower's grocery store. Darcy said her sitter would never notice she was missing.

They met in Mullet's yard and followed the tree-lined path to the community park.

"Listen, I'm going to go ahead so no one sees you with me," Darcy said.

A second later she was back. "Oh my gosh, you have to hide me."

"Duck behind Mullet's backpack, it's getting so big, it could hide a moose," Burt said.

Without another word, she lunged behind Mullet and crouched along behind them. Mullet started to turn to look at her, but she shoved him back.

"Don't look at me. Keep walking and look normal."

Burt tried to see who she was hiding from, but he didn't recognize any of the kids there. A few ladies with toddlers walked by, an old couple, and a few runners.

Finally, Darcy stood up. "Whew, that was too close. My aunt just ran by."

"Did she see you?"

"I don't think so."

"See," Mullet replied, poking his finger into Burt's shoulder. "You both keep getting annoyed with my big backpack, but it saved the day again!"

"It also gets in the way of everything," Burt said as they rounded the corner onto Main Street.

Burt and Mullet entered Hower's Grocery Store and weaved around the aisles until they reached Aisle Ten, with the peanut butter.

"I don't have any money on me," Burt said to Mullet as they stopped at the shelf filled with peanut butter and jelly.

"I have some emergency change in our detective pack for something like this," Mullet said as he swung the backpack around and unzipped the front pocket.

"Looks like there's enough to buy a candy bar," Burt said with a grin as he reached for the candy sitting on a nearby rack.

Mullet seized it out of his hand and put it back. "Detectives must be willing to give up their wants, tip number twenty-two in the "Detective's Guide to Being a Great Detective."

They wandered around the store until they heard the bell of the front door and waited for Darcy to find them. A minute later Darcy met up with them in the peanut butter section.

"We need to hurry; I saw Peter from school. He can't see me with you, or it will be the end of me. Get that cashew butter way up there. It isn't the good stuff that my mom gets online, but at least it looks nicer than that plain old peanut butter," she said as she wrinkled her nose and turned away.

"Bossy," Mullet whispered under his breath.

"Oh no," Darcy said as she ducked down at the end of the aisle and inched her eyes around the corner.

The sound of sneakers squeaked across the floor and Peter's annoying voice filled the aisle on the other side of them. Burt hurried after Darcy and crouched down beside her.

"Get away from me. What are you doing?' Darcy said through clenched teeth as she moved behind an enormous toilet paper display stacked almost to the ceiling with single-papered rolls of toilet paper. A sales sign read, "Buy two, get one free!"

"You have to buy the peanut butter," Burt said.

"What? Why do I have to buy it?" she said.

"We're broke," Burt said.

"Hey guys, look it here! I got the peanut butter! Ha! I may be short, but my vertical rocks!" Mullet yelled as he ran towards them. "Hey Darcy, catch!"

He jogged across the floor, tossing the peanut butter in her direction. Unfortunately, as he got closer, his feet tangled with the strap of his backpack, fumbled over each other, and launched him toward them. Darcy caught the airborne peanut butter, but not before Mullet smashed headfirst into them, launching all three into the entire toilet paper display.

Rolls of toilet paper sailed through the air and the entire toilet paper tower collapsed on top of them, leaving the once magnificent tower in a jumbled pile in the middle of the store.

Every single person in the store stopped and for a split second, everything was still.

Even though it didn't seem possible, Darcy's face was more furious than Burt had ever seen it. She jumped up, holding the peanut butter, and bolted to the front of the store.

Mr. Ben, the owner, reached them first. "Are you kids okay?"

The next person to round the corner was Peter, and he grabbed his stomach and started laughing and pointing. Mark, Danny, and the others joined in.

"Off you go, get out of here," Mr. Ben said as he shooed them away. He turned and gave Burt a friendly pat on the back, and nodded with understanding while Mullet explained that he had accidentally tripped. He'd owned Hower's grocery store for years, and his father, Jamie Hower, had owned the little store before him. Burt's mom said they stayed in business because they were so friendly, and Burt could see that Mr. Ben looked more entertained by Mullet's story than upset. They offered to pick everything up, glad to have an excuse to avoid Darcy.

It seemed like there were a million rolls of toilet paper to put back on the display, but it was almost worth it to attempt to recreate the coolest toilet paper tower ever. After they finished, they headed back to Burt's house, set up their lemonade stand, and waited for no customers to show up.

An hour into a customer-less afternoon they saw Darcy marching down the road.

"Great," Mullet muttered, "Just who I wanted to see."

They were silent as Darcy paraded up to their table and put her hands on her hips, glaring at them with a snotty expression on her face. Burt remembered feeling bad for her during the toilet paper incident, but now he wondered why he would ever feel sorry for someone who was always so rude.

"I have the peanut butter and I expect you to be at my house before three," she said as she spun around and walked away.

Burt looked at Mullet, who looked a little shocked.

"Have you ever heard anyone talk to someone like that?" Burt said

"No," Mullet said. "Who could have foreseen that we would land our first detective case and get stuck with someone like Darcy Bell?" he said as he rubbed his temples and closed his eyes.

"My dad always says that it takes hard work to earn money," Burt said.

"Guess so," Mullet said.

After a few minutes mourning their rotten luck, they poured themselves some lemonade and abandoned the stand to practice shooting hoops in Burt's driveway. Burt was slightly tall and husky for his age, and his strength helped him to hit those three-point shots. Today he was making almost everything he tossed up.

"If you keep doing that, you're going to get the summer MVP award," Mullet said.

"No, you're going to get it. You're quick and hit every layup before anyone knows where the ball is."

Mullet frowned. "I bet MVP goes to one of the silver spoons."

"We won't let that happen," Mullet said, tossing the ball into the air and hitting another basket.

At practice, Peter started laughing the minute they stepped out of Burt's van.

"That boy just has the cutest laugh," his mom said as she waved and smiled at him, which made Peter laugh even harder.

"You boys have fun," Burt's mom said, blowing them a kiss as she pulled out of the parking lot.

"Fun...right," Burt muttered under his breath.

"Look! It's the paper boys," Peter howled.

"Yeah, the toilet paper boys," Mark said.

"When they aren't taking out the trash, they like to play with toilet paper. Such unique talents," Peter continued. He didn't let up until Coach Clay arrived, and then continued to taunt them under his breath.

Burt couldn't believe Darcy actually spent her days at school hanging out with them. No wonder she was so paranoid. At least he and Mullet were tough and could outplay any of those guys any day on the court. The rich boys had a lot to say before practice, but once the basketball came out, it shut their mouths real fast. It didn't hurt that coach was coming around either. While he didn't favor Burt and Mullet, he was starting to look at them differently.

After practice, Mullet had to go to his own house. Mrs. Mullet said they were going to fuse together if they didn't spend some time on their own. There was nothing to do without Mullet. Since Jenna was five years older than him, she was kind of a bore and they didn't have anything in common. He played a card game with his mom and dad after dinner and then he headed outside to shoot some baskets.

Old Langley was out walking and stopped at the edge of Burt's driveway.

"Hey there! You got any of that lemonade?" he yelled.

"Lemonade?" Burt said.

"Yeah, need a whole pitcher of that lemonade of yours. I've got five dollars, son, what do you think?"

Five dollars! Burt's jaw dropped. "Sure, just a minute," Burt yelled.

He ran and grabbed a pitcher from the garage and ran back out. Old Langley looked like he would never be able to carry it, so Burt carried it for him. There were two cars in the driveway, and Mr. Langley explained that some family stopped by unexpectedly, and he had nothing for them to drink. He thanked Burt and headed inside.

Five dollars almost doubled their lemonade sales and, combined with the money from the peanut butter case, Burt could almost feel those new shoes on his feet. He called Mullet with the news and fell asleep dreaming of clouds and the SkyScrapers.

—Chapter 11—
PEANUT BUTTER WATCH

Today was the day—stakeout number two—and this time they were prepared.

After breakfast, they squeezed through the secret door of the clubhouse and noticed a folded piece of pink paper sitting on their makeshift desk.

"Oh boy, pink paper can only mean one thing," Burt said as he lifted it like his mom lifted used basketball clothes that had been sitting in his room for months. "Here, you touch it," he said, handing it to Mullet by a tiny corner.

"Gross, it smells like girl," Mullet said as he reached into the detective backpack and pulled out a pair of tweezers. He held them up and clapped them together. "In case we need to dust for prints." He carefully used the tweezers to unfold the note and read it out loud.

"Dear Detectives, the study window is open, you know where to find it. The peanut butter is in place. If you see me, which I hope you don't, don't talk to me," Mullet looked up at Burt. "Wow, she even sounds snotty when she writes. She didn't even sign her name."

"Do you think it's worth it?" Burt said, "Dealing with Darcy is one thing, and then there's the other thing about actually catching the peanut butter thief..."

"It's more money than we could make selling lemonade. Besides, someone in that house can't resist peanut butter. This is going to be our big break," Mullet said. "Plus, how many more practices can we go to with Peter calling us old town trash and toilet paper boys?"

Burt sighed. Part of him didn't want to go, but the idea of facing the team at practice after practice with duct-taped shoes was too much to bear.

Mullet picked up the backpack and headed out the door. Burt stood and followed him to the edge of Darcy's yard.

They waited while the gardener finished watering a set of rose bushes in the backyard. As soon as she finished and walked around to the other side of the house, they made a mad dash to the study window. Mullet grabbed the edge and lifted himself up, but got stuck on the windowsill by the bulky backpack. Burt heard the gardener coming back around the corner. He shoved Mullet through the window and then ran behind some flower bushes.

Mullet stuck his head out the window, saw the gardener, and quickly jerked his back in. Burt watched her walk around the edge of the yard, water flowers along a fence, and stop every so often to pull weeds and throw them into a bucket.

Mullet stuck his head back out the window and motioned for Burt to make a run for it. The gardener turned away, and Burt took a deep breath. He jumped up and sprinted for the window. Mullet grabbed him by the back of the shirt and hauled him through. They landed in a pile on the floor, laughing uncontrollably.

"That was close," Mullet said.

"Too close. But we didn't get caught. Now what?" Burt said.

"I guess we wait for Darcy."

"But she said she didn't want to see us. Don't you think we should try and get to the kitchen alone?" Burt said.

Mullet shrugged as Burt looked around the study. There wasn't a note or any sign of Darcy, so after several minutes, they decided to get into place themselves.

They carefully opened the door to the study and peeked out. They couldn't hear anything, so they crept through the halls until they came to the dining room.

"There's the door to the kitchen," Burt said to Mullet as they ducked beneath the dining room table.

"This way," Mullet whispered as he army crawled to the other side of the dining room and pointed to a set of doors. The doors were left slightly ajar, and Mullet left the cover of the table to crawl towards them.

Burt followed behind him and they both peered into Darcy's enormous kitchen. Mullet put his finger to his lips and pointed towards the far corner.

An elderly woman wearing an apron and tight bun was folding cloth napkins at the counter. He assumed she was the cook because he didn't recognize her. Mullet tapped Burt and pointed again. Burt looked around the room until he saw what Mullet was pointing at. The fancy jar of peanut butter from Ben's grocery store was sitting on the kitchen island.

Mullet made a writing motion in the air and pointed over his shoulder to the backpack. It took a second, but Burt finally realized what Mullet wanted. He slowly leaned forward, unzipped the detective pack, and pulled out the detective notebook, along with a pen. He handed them to Mullet. Within a few seconds, Mullet had two pages filled with notes.

The peanut butter was supposed to be in the cupboard, but now it was sitting out on the counter. Even though the cook was working just a few feet away from it, Burt could see that the lid was still screwed on tight. They continued to keep an eye on her, but it soon got boring watching her fold napkins and put them into a basket.

Even Mullet could think of nothing else to write about and set his pencil down with a huff.

After what seemed like hours, she finally finished folding the last napkin, stood up, and headed toward the dining room.

Burt and Mullet quickly scooted back beneath the table, hoping they were far enough under that she couldn't spot them.

Suddenly a bell rang and the cook sighed, turned, and went to the cupboard for a tray. On the tray went a teacup, tea, a spoon, sandwiches, and sugar.

Mullet's eyes lit up as she wrapped her hand around the jar of peanut butter. He jabbed Burt in the ribs with his pen and pointed.

"Ow," Burt said as they both leaned forward, holding their breaths.

To their disappointment, she put the peanut butter back into the cupboard without opening it and pulled out a box of cookies instead. She finished adding things to the tray and left the room. A few minutes later she came back and grabbed drinks from the fridge and disappeared again.

Mullet and Burt relaxed against the wall of the dining room.

"Any chance you think she's the thief?" Mullet said.

"I don't know. It didn't look like she was eating anything, but she might have eaten it earlier...Wait!

Maybe there's a spoon in the sink. Let's go find out," Burt said.

Mullet looked terrified at his suggestion. "I'm not sure it's worth the calculated risk."

"C'mon Mullet," Burt said, "If there is a spoon in there with peanut butter on it, then we've solved our case. Cook with the spoon in the kitchen. Done."

Mullet looked at the kitchen and then looked at Burt. "Okay you go in and check the sink, and I'll keep watch from here."

The floor creaked as Burt took his first step, and they froze in place.

"Shh, be sneakier," Mullet said.

"I'm trying," Burt said, starting to get agitated.

When Burt was sure he didn't hear anything, he tiptoed the rest of the way into the kitchen. His heart thudded against his chest, partly because he didn't want to get caught, and partly because he was hoping to find a peanut butter covered spoon sitting in the sink. Once he got to the sink, he stood and his shoulders drooped. There was nothing in the sink except for a dirty dishrag.

He heard a noise and spun around. Mullet was in the doorway, his eyes wide as he frantically waved him over. Burt hurtled toward the doorway of the dining room and attempted to skid to a stop as he tumbled into Mullet. They untangled themselves from each other as fast as they could, and frantically crawled back under the safety of the dining room table.

"I told you the risk-reward ratio wasn't in our favor," Mullet muttered under his breath.

The cook returned to the kitchen, set the empty tray in the sink, and headed to the dining room.

They slipped to the furthest edge of the table, praying that the cream-colored tablecloth hanging down from the sides was long enough to keep them hidden.

Soft hums filled the air as the cook made her way around the table setting the napkins out. She left again and returned with plates and silverware, bustling back and forth from the kitchen to the dining room, carrying more things than could possibly fit on the table. First, there were vases, then candles, more plates, salt and pepper shakers, and little white cards.

All they wanted to do was escape, but Darcy's mom came through the front door and began discussing all kinds of boring details about the dinner with the cook. Burt yawned and couldn't believe that they were stuck there listening to two old ladies chatter on about finger food and table settings.

"Hey Mom, someone's on the phone for you," Darcy said as she stepped into the room. She hesitated in the doorway as her eyes drifted to the corner of the table. "Oh, and Ms. Brown said she needed you both outside to decide what flowers you want cut for the bouquets," Darcy added, grabbing her mom and pushing her to the door.

"Alright Darcy, we're heading out, stop pushing us," Mrs. Bell said as she left the foyer with the cook trailing behind her.

The door slammed and small feet covered with fluffy pink socks made their way towards them.

"It's totally shocking that no one has caught you yet," Darcy said as she leaned beneath the table. "I could see your dirty shoes and that huge backpack sticking out from over a mile away."

Mullet pulled his backpack close to his chest. "Technically if you take the linear footage, you're not even a sixteenth of a mile away from us."

"I just meant that it's obvious that you are there."

"No one else saw us and that's what matters," Burt said as he started to climb out. He didn't dare admit to Darcy that she was right about Mullet's backpack sticking out.

She put her hands on her hips. "Did you find anything out?"

"Not yet, but there might be clues if can we get back into the kitchen," Burt said.

Darcy stepped back and peered out the window. "It is all clear right now, I bet they will discuss the flowers for the dinner for at least an hour," she said as she motioned them to follow her to the kitchen.

They clambered out from the table and rushed into the kitchen, all of them gasping at the same time.

"What is that?" Darcy said as she pointed to the open jar of peanut butter with a spoon sitting beside it.

"How did that happen?" Mullet said as he raced forward to examine it.

"That wasn't out there a minute ago," Burt explained to Darcy, "We were just in here and saw your cooking lady put it away, and somehow someone got it back out again."

"It must have happened while we were distracted by them talking about the dinner. This is a very blatant peanut butter thief to strike in broad daylight. I think we need to dust the jar for fingerprints," Mullet said as he pulled off the detective bag, unzipped it, and started pulling things out.

Soon a pile of binoculars, pens, miniature flashlights, matches, dog treats, and several books filled the counter.

"Geez," Burt said eyeing the pile of books, "No wonder that thing is so huge."

"Why do have so many books in there?" Darcy said as she lifted up a book about dragons.

"You never know what you'll come in contact with when you're a detective," Mullet replied, continuing to pull things out of the bag.

Darcy raised her eyes. "You think you're going to come in contact with a dragon?"

"After seeing your dad's study, I believe I could come in contact with anything." He reached to the bottom of the bag and looked up at them. "Oh no."

"What now?" Darcy said.

"We're missing the fingerprint dusting kit," Mullet said, a frown tugging at the corners of his mouth.

"How? I thought you had a list and checked it a million times?" Burt said

"I did, but I had to take everything out and repack it when I decided to add the dog treats and books in. I must have left it behind." Mullet looked completely defeated as he tossed everything back into the bag and zipped it up. He checked the front pouch and the sides. Finally, he fumbled through his pockets, pulling out all kinds of candy wrappers, gum wrappers, rainbow candies, and several packs of smashed Smarties.

"Wait a second! Darcy, do you have a paintbrush?" Burt said.

Darcy nodded as she walked over to a drawer, while Burt used the bottom of a water glass to crush the rest of the Smarties until they resembled dust.

Darcy turned around. "What are you doing? You're making a mess!"

"I'm making powder…"

"So that we can dust for fingerprints! Genius!" Mullet said, "Here, give me the paintbrush."

"You are going to get me in huge trouble. Our cook and housekeeper, Anita, just cleaned this kitchen," she said with a groan, but she handed him the paintbrush anyway.

Burt stepped aside as Mullet dabbed the paintbrush into the perfectly powdered candy. Even Darcy must have forgotten how angry she was, because she sat down and leaned forward, watching carefully as Mullet applied the powdery substance to the sides of the peanut butter jar.

The powder clung to it and Mullet blew on it lightly, revealing a clear fingerprint on the side of the jar.

"Woah," Darcy said.

Mullet continued to work on the rest of the jar, exposing several smudged fingerprints.

"Now that we've got fingerprints, can we find the thief?" Darcy said.

"Yes, now that we've got—" Mullet paused, his eyes widening. "Oh… oh no, it just occurred to me that our fingerprints are on there too, and the cashier's…"

"And Darcy's," said Burt.

"And the cook," replied Mullet.

"And whoever the thief is," finished Burt.

"Oh my gosh, it sounds like everyone touched it," she snapped, but before she could get angry, they heard the front door open.

"Someone's coming," Darcy said, "You have to get out of here! Hurry!"

They ran back into the dining room and dove under the table. Mullet left part of the backpack hanging out again, so Burt grabbed it and yanked it under the table just as someone walked into the kitchen.

"Darcy!" her mom yelled, "What have you done? Why have you left this trash all over the place?"

Mullet felt his pockets and looked up at the counter, where the wrappers he'd been collecting for months sat in a little pile.

"You made this huge mess and just after Anita cleaned it?" Darcy's mom continued. She stopped for a moment as her eyes zeroed in on the jar of peanut butter. "Have you been eating that peanut butter?"

"Mom," Darcy started.

"Don't you dare try to get out of it this time young lady! You know that I have peanut butter for you and that I have peanut butter for me. With having to downsize, I have to shop sales now to do this! You will pick up this mess at once and you will go to your room for the rest of the day!"

"But, I didn't make the mess or eat the peanut butter!" Darcy said.

"You're in here with the peanut butter and the spoon and a huge mess. That's it, Darcy! I am absolutely tired of the lies! No more dance. No more theater. No more ANYTHING until you get your act together!"

Tears rolled down Darcy's cheeks as she squeezed her eyes closed.

Darcy's mom swept Mullet's things into her hand and walked over to a cabinet beneath the counter and threw them in. She reached for a switch.

"That's not a trash compacter, is it?" Mullet whimpered.

A gruesome grinding sound echoed throughout the room.

With that, Mrs. Bell left and Darcy stomped away, leaving Burt and Mullet sitting below the table, listening to the harrowing death of Mullet's candy wrapper collection.

Without saying another word, they dashed like cowards to the study before Darcy could come and chew them out. They ran for Burt's house and hid in his room for the rest of the day.

—Chapter 12—
ANOTHER TRIP TO THE STORE

After too little sleep, they woke up the next morning and set up the lemonade stand. At least they had a business to fall back on when things got tough, they joked.

"I still can't believe she threw my candy wrapper collection away like it was trash," Mullet said. "My tape and string collection? Gone in one second, just like that," he said as he stared down the street.

The day dragged on forlornly, especially with Mullet mourning the passing of his pocket collections. Burt didn't say much either. They probably shouldn't have left without saying something to Darcy. He could see why she wanted to prove her innocence so badly. Her mom was nuts. It was obvious that Darcy wasn't the peanut butter thief, but his opinion wouldn't make her mom believe. They needed to find cold hard evidence, and they needed to find it fast.

Burt stood up. "We have to try again."

"Try what?" Mullet said. He'd had his head resting on the table and a dribble of drool stuck to his chin.

"We have to buy more peanut butter and redo the stakeout. We need stakeout two-point-oh. It's the only way. We were close and almost had the thief, I know it," Burt said. He reached down and pulled his shoes on, determined to make everything work.

"What about Darcy?"

"Leave that to me," Burt said, "C'mon, we can't waste any more time."

They took their precious, painstakingly earned lemonade money with them and walked to Ben's grocery store for the second time that week.

"There was a lot of peanut butter missing from the jar, right?" Mullet said as they walked.

"Yep," Burt said as he kicked a small stone along the sidewalk in front of him.

"But there was only a spoonful on the counter..."

"Right," Burt said. He stopped kicking the stone to focus on Mullet. "What is it?"

"I was thinking about it and I think the thief is a snacker. During the day they ate a spoonful, but at night, that's when they really eat it. That's it, that's when the thief is striking. Serious snackers come out at midnight to eat."

"You would know that, wouldn't you?" Burt said as he punched Mullet's shoulder. He would bet all the money in their jar that Mullet had some sort of snack stuffed into his pocket right now.

"It takes a snacker to know a snacker. Snacking is serious stuff. I think we need to be there at midnight to catch the peanut butter thief, not during the day."

Burt thought for a moment. "Wait, so if the thief eats it at midnight, then we can rule out some of our suspects, like the gardener and the housekeeper. I'd say we have to zero in on the family."

"Exactly, and I looked up the statistics and you would never believe the percentage of crimes committed by family members," Mullet said.

They stopped in front of the grocery store.

"Wait," Mullet said as he rummaged through the detective backpack. He pulled two pairs of blue medical gloves out of the first aid kit and handed a set to Burt.

"We're not leaving any fingerprints behind this time," he said as they headed into the store.

They went directly to the peanut butter aisle, where Mullet grabbed another jar of fancy peanut butter from the top shelf. They headed to the checkout and waited.

When it was their turn, the cashier reached for the peanut butter, but Mullet yanked it away from her and pulled out another pair of blue gloves. He held them out to her.

"Excuse me ma'am, but we are doing an experiment with this jar of peanut butter and respectfully ask that you put these on before you touch it."

She gave him an annoyed look as he dangled the plastic gloves in front of her.

At first, Burt didn't think she was going to put them on, but she looked between the two of them, sighed, and reached for the gloves. Shaking her head, she scanned the jar and placed it into a small paper bag. She took off the gloves and punched a few buttons.

"That will be nine dollars and sixty-three cents," she said.

"Ten dollars for a jar of peanut butter?" Burt said as he looked at Mullet, his jaw-dropping.

"You picked out the most expensive kind we carry," she said, "Would you like to trade it out for a cheaper one?"

"Oh no, this is good," Burt said. They would have to go through the whole process with the gloves all over again and their peanut butter thief definitely liked the expensive peanut butter.

Mullet already had the exact change counted out and handed her the money. "Thanks for your kind cooperation," Mullet said as he grabbed the bag.

The cashier chuckled as she handed them the receipt. "Good luck with your experiment."

They raced out of the grocery store and ran right into Mr. Ben. He smiled. "Well, if it isn't the toilet paper bulldozers excavating out my grocery store for the second time this week!"

"Sorry Mr. Ben," Mullet said.

"Don't worry! We didn't destroy anything this time!" Burt called as they continued running down the street.

They turned past the library, cut through the community park, and raced all the way to the headquarters. They collapsed on their logs and pulled off the rubber gloves.

"How are we going to get this to Darcy?" Burt said. After the last disaster, he really didn't know if he could ever face her again.

"We'll have to sneak back into her house," Mullet said.

"Without her knowing?" Burt said, "I don't think so. All the other times she invited us to sneak in, but if we sneak in without her permission… that makes us like…like robbers."

"Robbers steal stuff, we're leaving something," Mullet said.

"It has to make us some sort of criminal."

"Nah, it makes us like Robin Hood. We're doing something bad to do something good. Besides, we can't just march up to her house, ring the doorbell, and hand her the peanut butter," Mullet said.

"Actually, maybe we can," Burt said, taking the detective notebook and heading out the door.

"Wait up!" Mullet yelled as he chased after him.

Burt walked and stood in front of Darcy's house. For a moment he was feeling really confident, but now he wasn't so sure about his idea.

This was the first time they were going to use an actual door at her house. The walkway was lined with bright white and pink flowers, and the porch was spotless. There was a swing and several more pots of flowers everywhere.

Once they were in front of the door, he noticed a welcome mat that looked like no one had ever wiped their feet on it and pristine white paint. The white porch made their shoes look like the color of dirty dishwater.

"Do you really want to do this?" Mullet whispered.

"We have to," Burt said, and before he could run away and forget about his dumb idea, he pushed the doorbell.

They waited. Nothing.

"Alright, let's go," Mullet said, whirling around.

Burt grabbed the strap of his backpack and pulled him back. On the other side of the door, they heard rustling. The deadbolt unlocked and the door swung open.

"Hello. Oh! Oh my," Darcy's mom said, looking from their heads down to their worn-out shoes. She quickly erased the surprise from her face and gave them a pressed smile. "I'm sorry, I was expecting someone else. How may I help you?" She said.

Mullet just stood there, so Burt took over.

"Yes, um, we're here because we are doing a school...um..."

"A school newsletter!" Mullet blurted out.

Burt shot him a look, but now he had to go with it. "Right, our school has a newsletter, and I have here in my notes that our fellow schoolmate, Darcy, lives here... and we were wondering if, um, we could interview her?" Burt spit out as he pulled out his notepad and pen, and looked up at Darcy's mom. He gave her his biggest smile. Hopefully, she would fall for it.

"Right," Darcy's mom said as she backed into the door.

His spirits fell. He'd thought it was a good idea and his mom always said that no one could refuse his charming smile. He waited for her to slam the door in their faces, but to his surprise, she opened the door wider and waved them in.

"I'm sure Darcy would love to be interviewed. Let me go get her," her mom said. She turned and walked away, leaving them in the richly decorated foyer.

"Excellent," Mullet said as he pulled a brush out of the detective kit and started brushing an expensive blue vase that sat on a table beside the door.

"Mullet! Stop that," Burt scolded from under his breath.

"I bet there are fingerprints on here," Mullet said as he leaned towards the vase.

"Stop it before you blow our cover," Burt whispered, "We're not detectives right now, we're reporters."

Mullet turned around. "I'm the one who read 'The Detective's Guide to Being a Great Detective', all the way through from front to back, like it should be read. I know all about cover and I would never break it."

They heard footsteps approaching, so he shoved the brush into his pocket and stepped beside Burt.

Darcy and her mom came around the corner. Her mom looked pleased, but Darcy had a sour expression on her face and her hands were balled into fists. It was almost funny that she could be in a pink dress and bow, and look so scary at the same time. She stopped in front of them and folded her arms.

Darcy's mom introduced them, not knowing how they really knew each other.

"Alright, go ahead with the interview," Darcy's mom said. She looked at both of them and waited.

Burt glanced at Mullet. It looked like Darcy's mom was going to stand there and watch the entire thing.

"I, uh," Burt said as he fiddled around with his notebook. There was no getting out of this one. They were going to have to do an actual interview. He held his pen to the notebook and looked at Darcy. A good detective had to play his part, so he needed to be a good detective, or at least, appear like he was.

"We are here on behalf of Red Pine Elementary School, interviewing the fifth graders who graduated to middle school. We would like to ask you a few questions for the August edition of the school newsletter that will come out in… in…

"August?" Darcy said with an eye roll.

"Exactly! Would you mind getting interviewed?" Burt said.

Darcy made a face, but when she looked at her mom, her mom looked delighted.

"Wow sweetie, that's so wonderful getting interviewed for the paper! Go ahead," she said.

"Fine," Darcy said.

"First we'd like to ask you, uh," Burt started, but his mind went blank.

"About your summer activities, what wonderful activities are you doing this summer?" Mullet interjected.

Whoops. Definitely the wrong question.

Darcy's eyes narrowed into two little slits, reminding Burt of the scary crocodile in her father's study.

Mullet gulped and stared at his feet.

Why did Mullet manage to say the wrong things at the wrong time? They both knew why she wasn't doing any activities this summer, which is why they were standing in her foyer lying to her mother in the first place. How were they going to fix this now?

When Darcy didn't say anything, her mom answered. "Oh well, this summer we are going to Washington D.C. to learn about our nation's capital, aren't we Darcy?" Her mom said.

Darcy nodded.

"That's very nice," Burt said, "How very…educational of you."

Mullet stifled his laughter and then tried to cover it with a cough. Darcy's mother still looked pleased, and Burt thought he even saw the slightest smile on Darcy's face. He could do this. He was a good talker, he just had to figure out what to say.

"What do you expect to learn while you are there? The secret to Lincoln's assassination or if the president is allowed to take off his shoes in the oval office?" Burt said.

This time Darcy really did smile. "I don't know about Lincoln, but we are going to go on a tour of the

Whitehouse. If I see the president, I will ask him about his shoes," she said.

"Cool," Burt said. He was on a roll. "And how do you think you can use that experience towards your education?"

"I think it's important to know what the leaders of our country do, so we can contribute to our country as we grow up," she said.

Burt wrote in his notebook as Darcy's mom smiled proudly at her.

"As a previous fifth grader at Red Pine Elementary School, what advice do you have for the younger kids who will be there this fall?" Burt said.

"I would tell them to enjoy school and to do all the extra things like the science fair and the costume contest, and other things like that, because it makes school fun," she said. Her face grew very serious, and she added, "I would also tell them not to hang around only certain groups of kids. They should get to know everyone. It might surprise them who makes a good friend." She had a strange look on her face after she said it, which gave Burt the weirdest feeling, like he didn't want to hear the rest. Luckily, they were saved by the doorbell.

"Excuse me dears," Darcy's mom said as she stepped around them to open the door.

On the front porch stood Darcy's grandma and two of her aunts, holding large platters of food. They all hugged each other and started talking about their dinner plans for that evening.

Darcy's mom introduced them as the nice boys interviewing Darcy for the school paper.

Darcy's grandma turned to them. "Oh, that sounds so nice. I'd like to get a few copies of that paper for myself when it comes out."

"Of course," Darcy's mom said as she turned to them. "Do you think Darcy's interview will make the front page?"

"Mom!" Darcy said.

"Um," Burt said.

"It's just an interview. It's not that big of a deal," Darcy said.

Darcy's mom turned around. "It most certainly is a big deal and you gave such good answers. I would expect your reporter friends would love to see you on the front page."

"Of course," Burt said, trying to keep his award-winning grin from faltering.

"Say cheese," Mullet said, and something clicked and flashed.

Everyone turned and looked at him, even Burt, who had no idea where the camera had come from.

"We'll make sure that she makes the front page, especially now that we have a photo," Mullet said, giving them a thumbs up and putting the camera back in his bag.

Of course, Mullet would have a camera in their detective bag.

"We better get this food in the fridge," Darcy's aunt said, "Very nice to meet you, boys! I look forward to reading about my favorite little niece!"

Luckily, they all headed to the kitchen, leaving them alone with Darcy.

"Listen, if you still want our help, we have another idea," Burt whispered. "Meet you at headquarters in a few." With that, he grabbed Mullet and retreated before they could ruin anything else.

—Chapter 13—
HEADQUARTERS

They were high-fiving each other over their fake news article when Darcy burst in. Her face flamed so red that they braced themselves for the worst. But instead of yelling at them, she collapsed on the floor and started laughing.

"My whole family thinks I'm a star now that I'm going to be featured on the front page of the school newspaper, and they're discussing other places we could visit while we're in D.C. to make my next interview really shine," she said as she started giggling again.

"What are they going to do when the paper doesn't come out?" Mullet said.

Darcy's smile vanished.

Burt shot Mullet a look. How could he say something so dumb at a time like this? He might be smart with books and facts, but he had no tact sometimes.

"I don't know," Darcy said, frowning, "They're all planning on getting copies to frame. What am I going to do now?"

Suddenly she went from laughing to looking like she was going to cry. Burt wanted to smack Mullet's head. Sometimes he had the worst timing.

"Well," Mullet started, but Burt cut him off before he could destroy them even further.

"Don't worry. We're detectives and we take care of details like that, no problem. Let's worry about the peanut butter thief, and we'll fix the newspaper thing later," Burt said.

"Okay," Darcy said.

Mullet handed her the paper bag. She opened it. "You bought peanut butter? With your own money?" she said with surprise. She reached in to grab it.

"No!" they both shouted.

She dropped the bag. "What? What is it?"

"We can't get any fingerprints on it," Burt said.

"Oh, right. Good thinking," Darcy said. She picked up the bag and set it on her lap. "So, what's the plan now?"

"Mullet was thinking that whoever is stealing the peanut butter is stealing it at night," Burt said.

"Lots of crimes happen at night. Actually, statistics show that over fifty percent of crimes happen at night," Mullet added, puffing out his chest.

"But doesn't that mean there's still a fifty percent chance that someone is stealing it during the day?"

Mullet deflated.

"Anyways, we think we need to target your family. What about your brother? Is there any reason he would want to sabotage you?" Burt said.

"What?" Darcy said, "No, he wouldn't do that to me. Besides, he was at camp, remember?"

"Just because the crime was discovered while he was at camp, doesn't mean he didn't do it," Burt said.

"Think about it. What could be his motive? Maybe he's stealing the peanut butter to get you in trouble so he can ruin your whole summer," Mullet said.

"Why would he do that?" Darcy said, the color rising in her cheeks.

"Did you do anything to anger him, or make him mad? Brothers do things like that, maybe he's getting you back for something," Mullet added.

Darcy stood in a huff.

Clearing his throat, Burt spoke up, "I think what he means is, is there anything that your brother is upset about?"

"He says I'm a pain, but he would never ever try to ruin my whole summer. Not like this. The only thing he is upset about is the move," Darcy said. Her face turned red and then she stopped.

Burt glanced at Mullet and raised his eyebrows.

The pen was already poised in Mullet's hand.

"So, Darcy, can you explain why he is upset about the move," Mullet asked, stroking a fake goatee and attempting to sound understanding.

Burt glanced up at the tip list and found tip number forty-two…

Tip #42- Act understanding to get them to talk.

"Never mind," Darcy said, "What's the plan?"

Mullet put his pen down and stared at her over his notebook. "This may be important. Tell us about the move."

Darcy pursed her lips together. "I said, 'NEVER MIND.'"

Mullet dropped his notebook.

Burt reminded himself to make a note that tip number forty-two didn't work on girls… Or at least it didn't work on girls like Darcy.

The silence was filling the room faster than a fast break, so he scrambled to fix it. "Alright, so we think the criminal is most likely to hit at night, which means we were thinking we need to be there tonight to watch it happen," Burt said.

"Tonight is the dinner party, and everyone will be there, but how are you going to get in there without everyone seeing you?"

Burt grinned. "That's perfect. Everyone will be there, so we'll be able to nab the thief. We're the detectives, we'll figure out the details of how to not get seen." He looked at Mullet, waiting to see if he was going to say anything, but Mullet was still too stung to join the conversation. Burt was on his own. "Tell us about this party."

Darcy sat back down. "Most of the family is planning to stay the night. Obviously, my dad, mom, and brother are home. Both of my aunts and uncles are staying, and my grandma is staying. I have another aunt and uncle who are coming and bringing their kids, but they aren't spending the night. But I doubt it's them. They're busy and we don't see them very much."

"If we can stay for the first part of the night, then you can take over afterward and watch for the second part of the night," Burt said.

"No way," Darcy said, shaking her head and pointing her finger at them. "This is your job. I'm supposed to help entertain my little cousins. You will have to keep watch all night."

"But," Mullet said.

"You're the detectives, can't you handle a little detail like that?" Darcy said, mimicking Burt.

"We can because we're professional detectives," Burt spoke quickly, "What Mullet was trying to say is that's a lot of people, so how do we keep them all from seeing us? Plus, I'm guessing the dining room table is out this time."

He glanced sideways at Mullet, who was nodding vigorously.

"There is a cleaning closet that faces the pantry where we keep the peanut butter. It has little slits in the doorway, and no one ever uses it. Like, the cleaning lady does, but she won't be there. You can hide in there, but you should get there before everything gets too busy," Darcy said.

"But we can't just spend the night in your cleaning closet," Mullet said.

"You're the detectives, and you said you can handle anything, right? I'm giving you my allowance, so it's your job to catch the crook. If I'm the one who has to figure it out, then you can forget your whole detective contract," Darcy said as she turned to reach for it.

Burt's basketball reflexes kicked in, and he boxed her out, blocking her from the contract hanging on the wall. "No, no, no, no," Burt butted in, "We just need more time to figure out what to do about our moms."

They discussed their plans in detail as Mullet took notes. Darcy's part was ready. Now Burt and Mullet had to figure out how to make their part work. All three of them raced off in different directions, promising to meet back at the detective headquarters before five.

"Good luck!" Burt called to Mullet as he burst through his back door.

"Hey kiddo, are you having another great summer day?" his mom called from the kitchen.

He walked in and sat down on a stool at the counter. "Yep, but it would be even better if I could spend the night at Mullet's house," he said as he waggled his eyebrows.

"Again? Aren't you two getting sick of each other?" she said.

"Mom, we've been doing this since the first grade."

She shook her head and smiled. "I know. You're like brothers. Listen, it's fine with me if it's fine with Mullet's mom. And don't forget how lucky you are to have your best friend living next door."

"I know, Mom," Burt said as he dashed up to his room.

"And how lucky you are to have such a great mom," she called after him.

He ran around, trying to grab everything he would need. He changed into black sweatpants and a black long-sleeved shirt. He grabbed a navy cap and shoved a pair of sunglasses in his pocket.

He ran downstairs and gave his mom a quick hug.

"Why are you in long sleeves and pants? Where are the basketball clothes you live in all summer long? What are you doing, some sort of ninja stuff tonight?" she said.

"Sure Mom," Burt said, avoiding answering her thousands of questions as she rubbed his head.

He was the first one back to headquarters, so he sat on his log and grabbed the DGB. He turned to the section on being sneaky.

"Make sure you know the proper way to get around like a detective," he read out loud, "You must be on the lookout for items that make noise, like, twigs, leaves, newspaper, kid's toys, dog toys, etc. The best surfaces to walk on are carpet, soft grass, sidewalks, sand, and cement. Beware of squeaky floors, crunchy rock paths, dry grass, and trails with lots of debris."

The illustration showed a detective creeping along like a cat. It looked easy enough. Just as he was about to turn the page, Mullet squeezed through the secret door.

"Any good tips?" he said.

"Yeah," Burt said as he handed him the book. Mullet flipped through it for the hundredth time, while Burt checked out the backpack.

Darcy came in last. While they were in black from head to toe, she was in a brightly colored party dress with flowers all over it. Her hair was curled and pulled back with a big, flowered thing.

"You guys look *interesting*," she said.

"So do you," Mullet said, and Darcy stuck her tongue out at him.

"This is our detective gear," Burt said, not bothering to hide his annoyance. "People aren't going to be able to see us now with our dark clothes on, which is exactly what detectives are supposed to do. We blend into our surroundings."

Mullet pointed to the tips they had nailed up on the wall. "See number fifteen? A good detective always blends into their surroundings."

"What about your faces? They really stand out now," she said.

"Oh! That was on the list!" Mullet said. He grabbed the backpack away from Burt and searched through it. In a matter of seconds, the entire bag of detective items was strewn across the floor.

"Where did I put those?" he said, searching through the pile, and then through all of the pockets of the backpack. He turned the bag upside down and shook it again, but nothing else came out. He reached his hand into the very bottom, felt around, and looked up in dismay. Finally, he unzipped the front pocket.

"Here it is!" he said, holding up a small green box.

"Is that eyeshadow?" Darcy said.

"No," Mullet said, opening the lid to reveal three compartments of thick greasy-looking stuff. One was black, one was brown, and one was dark green.

"It looks like disgusting eyeshadow for guys," she said.

"My dad used to wear this hunting," Mullet said. He swiped his finger through the black paint and rubbed it across his face. "See?"

"Awesome," Burt said as he reached for the tin and spread the black and green paint all over his face.

Darcy tapped her foot and looked back towards her house. She looked at them and then looked back at her house again.

"What?" Burt said.

"While you two are getting your make-up on, time is ticking," she said.

"It's not make-up, it's camouflage," Mullet said.

"And it was your idea," Burt said.

"It was not my idea!" Darcy protested.

"Yes it was, you said that our faces were white," Burt said.

"I didn't tell you to smear them all with greasy gross make-up. You look like…" Darcy started.

"Hey guys!" a voice said.

They all swung around. Standing in the doorway was Tiana.

"Oh wow, you really are real detectives! Are you going on a top-secret mission or something?" she said.

"Yes. I mean, no. What are you doing here?" Burt said.

"I heard your voices and I wanted to see if you found my bracelet. I really want it back," she said.

"We're working on it," Mullet said, "But you need to get out of here. We're busy with official detective business, now scat!"

"I knew you were up to something! I can't wait to tell everyone when I get home! This is so exciting!" she said. She bent down and picked their official notebook up off the ground. "Oh cool, what's this?" she said as she opened it, completely disregarding the fact that it said, "Keep out or DIE!"

Mullet quickly swiped it from her hand and stuffed it into the backpack. Everything was out in the open and as fast as he tried to grab it, Tiana was faster, quickly snatching things off the floor and holding them away from him.

"Whoa, is this for fingerprints? You actually do that stuff?" she said as she held up their fingerprint kit.

Mullet reached for it, but not before she dropped it to pick up the magnifying glass, which she held up, magnifying her eyeball to the size of a grapefruit. "Cool!"

Burt grabbed it and tossed it to Mullet, who caught it easily and stuffed it in the bag. Her little hands were too fast for them though, swiping one thing after another as soon as they took each thing away.

Something had slid under the desk and she pulled it out in an instant. "Wow," she said as she held Mullet's camera up and took a picture. The flash went off, catching all of them off guard, nearly blinding them.

It took less than a second for Mullet to get it out of her hands. "Tiana, get out of here, okay? We have work to do."

"We'll talk to you about your bracelet later," Burt said as he grabbed her shoulders and guided her to the door.

"But I want to talk about my bracelet now," she said.

"Get out!" They all yelled.

She left and they breathed a sigh of relief. Even though she was only going into third grade, she was the busiest body on the block. Tomorrow they would have to figure out how to deal with her.

"I need to go," Darcy said, "Get to the study and I'll sneak you out once it's safe."

"Wait, there's one more thing," Mullet said, "Our guidebook says that soft grass is a quiet surface to walk on. Since the grass is so crunchy, could you turn on your sprinkler system for a few minutes?"

"Yeah," Darcy said, "I just have to hit a button to activate them."

They followed her to the edge of her yard where she had stashed a huge bunch of flowers sitting in a basket.

"Darcy!" her grandmother called, coming around the corner of their house.

Darcy picked up the basket. "Over here, grandmother! I was just picking you some flowers."

Burt was impressed. That was a pretty good cover for someone who wasn't a real detective. Now she had an excuse and everyone would think she was thoughtful. Maybe they should add that to the tips in the DGB.

—Chapter 14—
UNDERCOVER

The whoosh of the sprinklers was their first signal. Mullet peered out from the bushes to make sure the coast was clear and gave Burt a thumbs up... Tip number ten of their "Detective's Guide to Being a Great Detective."

Tip #10- Always make sure the coast is clear.

The yard was still, and they didn't see or hear anyone, although it was hard to hear anything with the whir of sprinklers going off.

Together they gave each other the secret signal, a tap on the nose, and then took off towards the study window.

Everything was going perfectly until Griffin bounded out of the flower bushes. Mullet screamed and skidded to a stop.

That was all the dog needed. He lunged for them and they both took off around the back of the house. They rounded a corner and tried to stop, but the grass was so wet from the sprinklers that they slid across the yard like an overly waxed basketball court.

There was nothing they could do to stop themselves before they reached the arc of the sprinklers, and slid, finally landing in a puddle of mud. Griffin darted around the edge of the sprinkler system, and jumped on them, licking their faces.

"Get off, you stupid dog," Mullet said as he tried to push Griffin away.

Griffin lifted his long snout into the air and sniffed. He opened his mouth widely, latched onto the detective backpack, and started tugging. Mullet waved his arms, trying to get Griffin to quit, but his struggles only provoked the dog into a game of tug-of-war.

"Help!" Mullet yelled as the sprinklers chittered around them.

Burt pulled himself up and managed to wrestle the strap out of Griffin's mouth. Griffin barked and attacked Mullet's sweatpants. Burt managed to grab onto the dog's collar and tried to pull him away. Finally, Mullet reached into his pockets and pulled out two handfuls of beef jerky, and chucked them across the yard.

With Griffin distracted, they finally got a good look at each other. They were sopping wet, and covered in mud and grass clippings. The dripping paint on their faces made it look like they had been through a rough Halloween night.

Burt wiped his grassy hands on his sweatpants. "That was all about beef jerky?"

"There goes our snack," Mullet said.

"Now what? We'll leave grass and mud everywhere if we go into Darcy's house now," Burt said.

"And we'll have no beef jerky to snack on either," Mullet added miserably. He held up the backpack and water dripped from it. They heard the sprinklers stop.

"We can't stop now. We've been through too much," Burt said.

"I don't know," Mullet said as he looked at their clothes.

"Detectives don't give up," Burt said, "And we can't either. Right now there is a peanut butter thief eating dinner with Darcy and letting her take the blame. We told her we would help her and we will. Plus, we *need* those shoes."

He was so determined that Mullet couldn't argue with him. He was right, after all the trouble they'd gone to, they couldn't give up now.

They would have to make do with their wet clothes, but a good detective improvises. Even though the sprinklers were done, they still had to deal with Griffin.

Mullet called for him. He pulled a plastic bag of food out of the backpack and dumped the entire bag on the ground.

Smashed toaster tarts, cheese crackers, popcorn, and candy littered the ground. Griffin sniffed at the food and started to lick the toaster tarts.

"I thought you said our food was gone."

"That was the backup supply, now it's really gone," Mullet said sadly.

"It's for a good cause," Burt said as he patted him on the back. "I'd starve for days for those SkyScrapers."

"Me too," Mullet said.

They shuffled clumsily across the wet grass and finally, after what seemed like forever, made it to the window without any other incidents. Mullet pulled himself through first and turned around to help Burt through.

"The DGB didn't mention being a good detective would be so hard," Mullet said through heavy breaths.

"There's a lot of things that it forgets to mention," Burt said.

They flopped on the floor in exhaustion. They were already worn out and the night hadn't even started yet.

"I think this calls for a snack," Mullet said as he reached into his pocket.

"I thought you gave all the snacks to the dog?"

"Nope. I still got this," he said as he held up a miniature chocolate bar with triumph.

It was the size of Burt's small pinky, but they split it anyways and celebrated their successful excursion getting into the house.

A moment later, their stomachs growled, and they were back to mourning their long night with no foreseeable food in the future.

To make matters worse, delicious smells wafted from the dining room, and they had to sit there with sopping wet clothes, while they smelled it.

After what seemed like hours of antagonizing torture, the door to the study opened, and Darcy poked her head in.

"Where have you been? I waited in here after I started the sprinklers and you never showed up. You could have ruined everything!"

"I have no response to that," Mullet said, giving Burt a look.

"Oh, I have to go," Darcy said as someone called her name. The door clicked shut and they were left alone in the creepy study again.

"This place gives me goosebumps," Mullet said, scooting closer to Burt.

Burt nodded, trying to avoid the murderous eyes of the devil bear in the corner. He kept his eyes wide and alert as he peered around the room trying to avoid the gleam of the boar's tusks and the teeth of a coyote. Even the head of the whitetail deer had a menacing look in the shadows.

There was a scratching sound and they jumped at the same time.

"What was that?" Mullet whispered.

Someone had to be brave and Burt knew it wasn't going to be Mullet. "It was probably just a tree branch scraping the side of the house," Burt said.

"Are you sure? Because I don't remember any trees by the house. I'm starting to wonder if these animals are coming to life," he said as he looked around nervously.

Another scratching sound came from the side and they both darted beneath the pillows of the couch.

"I hate this place… it's like an animal morgue and I feel like their dead souls are coming after me," Mullet's muffled voice said from under the cushion.

The door opened and the light flicked on.

"What are you doing?" Darcy hissed, "You're supposed to be ready to go, not hiding under the couch pillows." She walked over lifted the pillow off of Burt's head and whacked him with it.

"We heard noises," Mullet said as she rounded on him.

Darcy rolled her eyes. "It was probably just my cousins. Let's go."

They stood up from behind the couch and she gasped.

"What happened to you?" Her eyes roamed from their clothes, to their shoes, and to the floor where they had been sitting.

"We had an issue with the sprinklers," Burt said.

"And the dog," Mullet added.

"Ugh, I seriously have to do everything?" Darcy said, "I'll go find you some clothes and you better get this mess cleaned up before I get back."

With the light on, they found a box of tissues and used the entire box to wipe up the grass clippings and watery mud they tracked everywhere. Darcy returned and threw them a bag of clothes and shut the door.

Mullet opened it. "Uh uh. No way."

Burt grabbed the bag from him and looked inside. Folded at the bottom of the bag were two pairs of sweatpants with matching sweatshirts.

One set was pink and the other one purple.

"We've come this far," Burt said as he stripped off his black sweat suit. He took out the pink set and pulled them on. The pants stopped right above his ankles.

"If anyone sees us in this," Mullet threatened as he pulled the purple sweatshirt over his head, "I'm running away—probably to Africa." Even though the small sweatshirt didn't cover his entire belly, he stretched it down, only for it to snap back up. He stretched it down again, but it flung up again, resting right at his belly button. He looked up at Burt. "I can't do this."

"No one will see us," Burt said as he attempted to hike his pants up higher to diminish the gap between his top and the pants. "Remember? We're detectives. We owe it to Darcy and we can adapt to anything…even Darcy's girly sweatpants."

"I don't know," Mullet said as they stared at each other.

Even though Burt had an older sister, he had never seen anything quite like Darcy's sweatpants. Mullet's purple shirt had a fluffy kitten with long white fur and with a gemstone collar, and Burt's pink one had ballerinas with actual tutus that stuck out. Pink glitter seemed like it was coming from everywhere. Every time he moved, glitter exploded from his sweatshirt.

The door opened as Mullet stuffed their wet clothes into the backpack. Darcy saw them and started to giggle.

"Don't. Say. Anything," Burt warned.

"No need," she said as she turned and waved them out the door.

They crept along the hallway behind her. Burt was glad to be out of that dead animal room, even if he was wearing pink sweatpants.

They continued down the long hallway until they came to the cleaning closet that faced the kitchen. Darcy opened the door and motioned for them to get in.

The closet wasn't necessarily small, but it wasn't exactly roomy either due to the way the shelves were situated. The side walls had all kinds of hooks with mops, brooms, and brushes hanging from them, and the whole space reeked of bad lemon.

"It smells like nasty lemon fart," Mullet said.

"Deal with it," Darcy said as she shut the door on their faces.

"She's not very understanding, is she? I thought girls were supposed to be nicer," Mullet said through a pinched nose.

There was just enough room to stand, but Burt's legs were already cramping. He tried to move around Mullet, but the backpack was in the way.

"Mullet, if you move that way and I move this way, maybe we can make enough room to sit down."

They shuffled around each other and with the quick replacement of a few buckets and cleaning supplies, they managed to make enough room to sit below the first shelf.

The detective backpack rested on Mullet's legs, but it was bulky and in the way, and some sort of sharp object was poking into Burt's side.

"Mullet, your stupid backpack is crunching me," Burt said. He shoved it away and Mullet shoved it back. Burt shoved it back towards him. Mullet pushed it back.

"Mullet," Burt said through clenched teeth, "We need to do something about this backpack before I clobber you over the head with it."

"THIS backpack is important," Mullet said. "It has everything we need in it."

"Everything but food," Burt said.

They glared at each other.

"Fine, I'll put it up," Mullet said. It took a lot more maneuvering and shushing, but he finally managed to get the backpack hung on a hook on the wall beside them.

"I hope for your sake, we don't need anything in there," he said.

Burt took a deep breath. This was not the time to fall apart. "And now we wait."

"And now we wait," Mullet echoed as he peered through the slits.

—Chapter 15—
THE BROOM CLOSET

After waiting and waiting for something to happen, they heard footsteps enter the crime scene. A rush of adrenaline coursed through them. But their excitement was dashed when they recognized the fluffy pink socks striding across the room.

"I hope you are both paying attention to everything," Darcy said as she marched up to the door and pulled it open.

"Don't you realize you could jeopardize the whole case by doing that?" Mullet said.

"Fine," Darcy huffed, "I was going to bring you something to eat, but I'll just take the leftover food from the party and stick it in the fridge." She snapped the door shut and walked away.

Burt reached up and twisted the handle, and shoved the door open with his foot, "Come back."

She turned around and glared at them. They marveled at the plate of food sitting in front of her piled with meatballs, garlic bread, and mini cheesecakes.

"We're sorry," Burt said, his mouth-watering.

She turned and looked at Mullet. When he didn't say anything, Burt elbowed him and tilted his head toward the food.

"Sorry," Mullet muttered.

"I didn't hear you, Mullet," Darcy said, "Did you say something?"

"Sorry," Mullet sputtered out, sounding like he was in immense pain.

Darcy reluctantly walked back and handed over the food. They thanked her, and even Mullet sounded sincere once the food was in his hands.

"Listen, the games are almost over, and my cousins are getting ready to leave. I'm not sure what the adults will do, but when I have a chance, I'll come back and join you," Darcy said.

"What?" Mullet said as he choked on the piece of garlic bread he'd just put in his mouth.

"I'm joining you. I want to catch the thief way more than you do." She stared at them for a second. "Don't look at me like that. Whoever is stealing the peanut butter is ruining my summer, not yours," she snapped.

Burt could argue that he wanted to catch the thief as much as she did. If she had to endure the teasing they did, she probably couldn't handle it. Not having cool shoes would ruin her summer too, especially since she was used to having everything she wanted.

"We smell from the mud and there's hardly any room in here," Burt said, trying to come up with anything he could to steer her away.

"There'll be more room if I take this," Darcy said.

Before either of them had a chance to protest, she reached down and yanked their detective backpack off the shelf, shut the door, and walked away.

Mullet stared out the door with a dumbfounded look on his face. He could barely swallow his food. "She took my backpack," he finally managed to squeak out. "What if we need it? What are we going to do? The very first tip of the guidebook says to always be prepared. It says *always*," he said.

"It also said that wet grass was a good surface for a detective to walk on. Look how that turned out," Burt said as he pointed to the cat on Mullet's sweatshirt.

"Just so you know, you have pink glitter all over your face," Mullet muttered.

They looked at each other for a moment and then had to look away, trying not to laugh. Once they knew they could keep the laughter in, they continued to eat until all the food was gone.

***

Burt flipped the notebook open and sketched a map of the soon-to-be crime scene. For now, everything was quiet except for the scratching of his pencil against the paper. He couldn't be sure, but he didn't remember the guidebook mentioning anything about how long detectives had to wait for something to happen.

"Do you hear something?" Mullet whispered after a while.

Burt leaned forward and leaned his ear against the door. Something was creeping lightly across the floor.

"It's either Darcy or a mouse," Burt said.

Sure enough, pink fuzzy toes appeared through the slits of the doorway. They stopped for a moment as her shadow twisted back and forth, and then straightened. The pink feet crept forward.

The doorknob turned ever so slowly. Darcy opened the door and put a finger to her lips. She stepped into the closet, squished herself between them, and shut the door.

"See anything yet?" Darcy said.

"Only pink fuzzy socks that remind me of Sasquatch," Burt said.

"Shut up," Darcy said as she sat down.

"Ouch! Your elbow is in my side," Mullet said.

"It's a tight fit," Darcy said as she wiggled around.

"You're telling me," Burt said as her elbow slammed against his face. His knees were up to his chin, his left arm was smashed against the shelf, and his foot was pinned against the door.

"Ow, you're hurting me," Mullet said as Darcy continued to squirm. "Everything was fine until you came."

"I told you, I want to see who the thief is too," Darcy said. She suddenly grew still.

They could hear someone walking down the hallway. A pair of feet with white socks came into view and then disappeared. Water gushed from the faucet. The water stopped, and before long, the whistling of a kettle pierced the air. There was more clinking and moving, the whistling stopped, and whoever it was left.

"Who was that?" Mullet said.

"It's probably my mom, she always makes tea at night, especially when she's with people," Darcy whispered.

"What's everyone else up to?" Burt said.

"My cousins left and my grandma went to bed, but my aunts and uncles are still playing cards with my parents. They're probably just sitting around and talking now. I don't really know where my brother went, but maybe I should check."

She stood then, elbowing and squishing them in the process. Not bothering to be sneaky or spyish or anything, she hurried across the kitchen, leaving the door to the closet wide open.

"She's going to blow our cover," Mullet said as he started to get up.

Right then, someone else walked into the room and he froze.

"Hey girlie, I thought you were in bed," Darcy's aunt said.

Mullet about lost it.

Her aunt's back was to them, but all she needed to do was turn around and they would be caught for sure. Burt didn't dare move anything, not even his eyelashes which were now squeezed tightly against his cheeks as he waited for the inevitable to happen.

Darcy's voice sounded panicked at first, but then she played it cool. "I was in bed, but decided to come look for a snack," Darcy said.

"You're still hungry after all that food?" her aunt said.

"A girl's got to eat," Darcy said.

"That's true, especially if she's in sports. Are you still in dance and theater? And doesn't soccer start soon?" her aunt said.

"Yes. I am hoping to try out for the theater program and dance. But I don't think it's really a sport. At least, not like all the running you do," Darcy said.

"Dancing counts! You move around and sweat and burn lots of calories," Darcy's aunt said with a grin, "So what's the best thing to eat in here?"

"I don't know, I was just starting to look," Darcy said as they both stuck their heads into the pantry.

Burt's foot was falling asleep, so he slowly started to move it over. Mullet shook his head back and forth and looked so alarmed that Burt stopped it midair. He remained still as Darcy pulled out a box of cheese crackers and showed them to her aunt.

"Yeah, those don't have that much protein in them, or really anything that great for you," Darcy's aunt said, examining the ingredient list. "Protein is what you want, it helps repair your muscles after you work out. Maybe I'll just get some chocolate milk, do you want any?" Darcy's aunt said.

"No thanks." Darcy's voice squeaked as her aunt turned sideways.

They could see the profile of her face in the light of the fridge. She moved things around as she talked, but Burt hardly paid attention. Every time her head bobbed above the door, his heart pounded, knowing they were about to get caught.

Burt caught Darcy's eyes, and he mouthed something. Darcy's face crinkled and he mouthed it slowly again. Darcy held her hands up in the "what are you saying" position.

Mullet didn't move, but Burt slowly lifted his hand and pointed to the closet door. Darcy shook her head.

"Aunt Lizzie, you're our guest. Why don't you go back to the living room and I will bring milk and a tray of cookies for everyone too," Darcy said.

"What a sweet thing to say, but you don't have to do that," her Aunt Lizzie said.

"I insist," Darcy said as she grabbed the jug of milk from her aunt, set it on the counter, and escorted her out of the room.

It didn't occur to either of them to shut the door until Darcy came running back.

"What are you doing? Why didn't you shut this? I gave you the perfect opportunity!" Darcy said as she hurried towards them.

"You're the one who left it open," Mullet said.

"But then I had to get rid of my aunt. You should have shut it then. Maybe I should just forget about my summer. This will never work," Darcy said, her shoulders drooping.

Suddenly Burt felt bad for her. When she was talking to her aunt about dancing and theater her whole face lit up. She seemed to love it as much as they loved basketball, and he couldn't imagine being away from basketball for an entire summer, even if it meant going without cool shoes.

"The peanut butter thief seems to like their peanut butter; he is bound to strike again. We'll catch him, I promise," Burt said.

Darcy nodded but didn't look very hopeful, and she closed the closet door and ran into the kitchen. She put together a plate of cookies and started to pour a glass of chocolate milk.

"What are you doing, kid? Talking to yourself?" Darcy's brother, Hank, said as he entered the kitchen.

"There's nothing wrong with talking to yourself," Darcy said.

"Sure, as long as you don't mind sounding crazy," Hank said as he made a crazy face and stuck his tongue out at her.

"Whatever," Darcy said.

"What do you have there?" he said pointing to the cookies.

"They're for the family, not for you," Darcy said as she tried to push around him.

"Hey, calm down. I was just asking. You've been so moody lately and not any fun. I was just coming to get some crackers and peanut butter, so I'll leave you and your cookies alone."

Darcy dropped the entire platter of cookies when he said the word "peanut butter."

***

"Wow, you crazy klutz," her brother said with a laugh as he bent down and started picking up cookies.

"Shut up, it's not funny. I'll clean it up," Darcy said as she reached down and picked up the platter, eyeing him as he reached into the pantry.

"So much for helping," he said as he stopped and stood.

Darcy eyed him as she reached into the pantry and grabbed a box of crackers with one hand and the jar of peanut butter they bought from the store with the other.

This was it, this was their big moment. They were finally going to crack the case and were on their way to new shoes as soon as Darcy handed over her allowance.

Darcy stood frozen in place with her mouth hanging open as her brother grabbed a plate and a butter knife. He dumped the crackers onto the plate and unscrewed the lid of the peanut butter.

"Ah yes, a new jar. It literally tastes the best when it's a brand-new jar and no one has scooped anything out of it yet," he said.

There was nothing she could say but only watched with wide eyes.

He lifted the jar to his nose and breathed in the smell. Reaching for a cracker, he sunk it into the peanut butter and shoved it in his mouth. Then he gagged and ran to the sink, blowing chunks of cracker and peanut butter out of his mouth. He turned the faucet on to run his mouth under it.

"Ugh, that's about as gross as your cookies," Hank said as he grabbed the chocolate milk Darcy poured and chugged it, "Mom and her fancy nut butter, yuck. I don't know how she eats that stuff. Give me plain peanut butter and that's it."

"You mean, you don't like it?" Darcy said.

"Are you kidding me? That stuff's disgusting," Hank said as he lifted the jar and read the label. "Cashew butter with coconut oil, Madagascar vanilla, cinnamon, and no added sugar. Gross."

Darcy walked over to her brother and stuck her finger in the jar. She put it in her mouth and sputtered.

"Ew! What's in that stuff?" she said.

"You don't like it either? I thought you were the one in trouble for eating all of Mom's fancy peanut butter. The super expensive healthy stuff that mom gets tastes like puke," Hank said.

"So, if you're not eating it, and I'm not eating it, then who is eating it?" Darcy said.

"Beats me. Maybe it's the dog, he eats anything," her brother said.

"Not anything," Burt whispered, thinking of the peanut butter cookies.

Hank grabbed some chips from the pantry, punched Darcy's shoulder, and headed out of the kitchen.

Darcy's face flushed. Burt thought she would be happy that her brother wasn't stealing the peanut butter, but she looked kind of upset.

After she picked the rest of the cookies off the floor, she turned her attention toward them. That's when Burt realized that she wasn't sad, she was mad. She stomped over to them and plopped down, purposely elbowing them as she wedged herself between them.

"What's your problem?" Mullet said as he nudged her away from him, which bumped her into Burt.

She rammed her shoulder back into Mullet's. Mullet shoved her even harder, and Burt's entire body felt like a punching bag as they pummeled each other back and forth.

"Both of you stop," Burt said, "You're hurting me."

"Who cares," muttered Darcy.

"Blame her," Mullet said.

"What is going on? Aren't you glad that your brother isn't the thief and we've eliminated another suspect?" Burt said.

"You guys turned me against my own brother, and he isn't even the thief. He doesn't even like that stuff. I've been mean to him ever since you suggested that he could be the thief," she said.

"We didn't make you accuse him. We just made a suggestion, and that's that," Mullet said.

Darcy folded her arms, refusing to talk to either of them.

That was fine by Burt. At least they couldn't get caught if they were all silent. The time ticked by slowly. Burt's stomach growled, but he didn't say anything as Darcy sat like a statue, her face set in a frown and her arms crossed over her stomach. Mullet sat the same way.

Burt's stomach continued to grumble. He willed himself to stop it, but no amount of willingness would make it stop.

Darcy broke out of her statue face. "Everyone in the whole house is going to hear that," she hissed.

His stomach roared again and was echoed by Mullet's.

"Seriously why does it sound like you have a bowling alley in your stomachs?" she said.

"It's secret detective language. When you have to keep your mouth shut, you communicate with your stomach," Mullet said. He kept his face serious, and Burt had to look down to keep from laughing.

"Well, if you don't stop, you're are both going to get us caught with your stomachs competing for the loudest rumble," Darcy said in an annoyed voice. She opened the closet door and walked into the kitchen while their stomachs continued to growl.

"For real, I can hear it all the way from here. It's worse than my dad's snoring. Don't you have some detective rule to make it stop, like eat a Tums or something?" she said.

"It's called food," Mullet said.

"I'm getting food," she said as she leaned into the pantry, making a bunch of racket. Something fell and rolled across the kitchen floor.

Mullet leaned towards Burt. "She's the one who is going to get us caught making all that noise! And she grumbles way louder than our stomachs do!"

"Be nice, there's food involved," Burt said.

Mullet frowned.

"Do it for the shoes," Burt whispered.

"For the shoes," Mullet said as he gave Burt a fist bump.

"For the shoes," Burt repeated, knowing somehow those shoes were going to get them in big trouble.

Darcy seemed calmer when she returned to the closet with three sodas, the plate of cookies, and some sandwiches. Mullet took the platter and Burt closed the door behind her.

"Hurry up. Something needs to shut your bellies up," she said. She didn't necessarily sound nice, but she didn't sound as mean either.

Mullet grabbed a cookie. "Are these the cookies you dropped on the ground?"

"It's all that's left," Darcy said.

"Fine with me," he said as he stuffed one in his mouth.

As soon as they started eating, their stomachs quieted down.

They waited for the thief, but no one showed up. Again, nothing in the guide had mentioned anything about the agonizing thing called waiting. This was supposed to be an exciting stakeout, but detective work was starting to feel boring.

Just when Burt decided he was going to die of boredom, they heard footsteps again. These steps were heavy as they thumped the ground. It was Darcy's dad. He opened the fridge, grabbed something, and left.

Burt sunk his head, all that hope and waiting for nothing. When was the thief going to show up?

A few minutes later, there were more footsteps. Darcy's mom and two aunts walked in. They chatted as they made tea. The kettle whistled and their spoons clinked against their teacups as they stirred sugar to them. Soon the kitchen was quiet once again.

"Oh! I forgot to turn the stove off," Darcy's mom called as she rushed back into the kitchen to turn off the burner. She turned around and started to walk away when Mullet burped. She stopped and looked around the kitchen.

They were all as silent as could be, but she was a mom with that mom radar that can detect anything… another tip the detective guide didn't mention. She put her hands on her hips and tilted her head, and then to their horror, walked over to the cleaning closet.

—Chapter 16—
CAUGHT

Darcy's mom put her hand on the doorknob and twisted. Burt closed his eyes. He couldn't watch. Everything seemed to happen very slowly. The doorknob clicked. The door creaked open, and, for a split second, everything was completely silent.

Then she screamed so loudly that they all screamed too. Mullet shot up and banged his head on the shelf above them. The shelf wobbled up and down and then toppled onto their heads, dumping buckets, rags, and cleaning products all over them.

"What? What is this?" Darcy's mother said, "Darcy! What on earth is going on?"

None of them moved. It didn't matter that Burt was covered in a pile of rags, or that Mullet had a bucket on his head. None of them were ready to move, especially considering the look on Darcy's mom's face.

"Darcy Louise Bell, I demand an answer right now," her mom said sternly.

Darcy crawled out from the pile of cleaning items. "I was just, we were just," she started.

Just then Darcy's aunts ran into the room to see what all of the commotion was about. As soon as they saw the look on their sister's face, they froze too.

"Darcy, I am waiting for an explanation on why you are stuffed in the closet at midnight with two boys I don't know," her mom said through gritted teeth. By now Mullet had the bucket off his head, and she took a good look at them. "Wait a minute, are you the boys from the school newspaper? Get out here, right now."

A funny look crossed her face as they crawled out of the closet. "Why are you wearing my daughter's clothes?"

Burt looked down. He had completely forgotten they were wearing Darcy's sweatpants. He looked over at Mullet, who was in the kitty sweatshirt revealing his whole belly and watery paint smeared all over his face.

"Well, you see, Mrs. Bell," Mullet said as he tried to yank the kitty shirt over his stomach. It shot back up, so he pulled it down again and held it in place as he talked. "We realized we needed a little more detail for our article…We uh… needed to feel like we were in Darcy's shoes. You know, really get a picture of her life."

"Then why didn't you just try on her shoes… at a normal time of day?" She said through clenched teeth.

Burt and Mullet looked at each other. They didn't have any answer for that.

She turned back to Darcy with disbelief. "Of all the crazy things, Darcy."

Aunt Lizzie took a step forward. "Sis, you are scaring these boys to death."

Burt wanted to nod in agreement but didn't dare under the dreadful gaze of Mrs. Bell.

"Get out," Mrs. Bell said.

"Oh, don't be so harsh with them, they're just kids," Darcy's other aunt said.

Mrs. Bell's head snapped to her sister. "Don't you dare tell me that I shouldn't be mad about finding my twelve-year-old daughter stuffed into a closet with two boys in the middle of the night," she shrieked.

Burt and Mullet took a couple steps back. "Sorry Mrs. Bell," they mumbled as they stared at their feet. Her eyes bored into them.

Darcy found her voice again. "Mom, we just thought that we would…"

Suddenly Aunt Lizzie started laughing, "What? Pull some sort of prank?"

All of them stared at her. Darcy's other aunt started to laugh too. Darcy's mom, on the other hand, didn't even crack a smile. In fact, her lips didn't twinge at all.

"This isn't funny," she said, "There is no reason why Darcy should be sneaking boys in here in the middle of the night."

Suddenly Mullet lit up. "We were just going to help Darcy play a prank on her brother, you know scare him a little."

"Those outfits you have going on would definitely scare him," Aunt Lizzie said as she laughed even harder.

Darcy joined in. "Yeah. You know how he always picks on me. When I got to know our newspaper reporters, I thought we would get him tonight. It was just for fun, Mom. I didn't mean anything by it."

The glare on her face didn't soften. This was it… they were in really big trouble.

"Oh Lane, they're just kids, they're just having fun," Aunt Lizzie said.

Ignoring her sister, Darcy's mom looked at them pointedly. "You boys need to get home now. Any pranks you play for fun need to happen during daylight hours, and not in my kitchen in the middle of the night. I'll have to think of another punishment for you, young lady. As for you two, I don't want to see you over ever again without an invitation first. Not even to deliver that newspaper of yours."

She grabbed their arms and led them to the front door. Neither of them resisted as they mumbled apologies one more time before she slammed the door shut on them. They walked silently down the sidewalk in their girly pajamas all the way to Burt's house.

The front doors were locked.

"Better go around back," Burt said.

The back doors were locked too, so they headed over to Mullet's house to find that his doors were locked too.

"I have a house key, but it's in the backpack," Mullet mumbled, "What are we going to do now?"

Burt thought for a moment. "How about we sleep at headquarters? It's warm and didn't you put a few old blankets in there for an emergency?"

Mullet's face brightened. "Yeah, I did."

They turned back and walked to Old Langley's house. The shed was cozy. They pulled the blankets around them and laid down.

"Our detective bag," Mullet said miserably.

"We'll get it back," Burt said.

"If I had the bag, then I would have the key to my house," he said.

"I know," Burt said.

"I also had mini pillows, flashlights, and pepper spray to keep stray dogs away… If we had the bag we wouldn't have needed that stuff anyway, because I would have had a key, and we'd be sleeping in my room where we were supposed to be sleeping to begin with."

"I know," Burt said.

"And we didn't even catch the thief," he muttered.

"Maybe it is the dog," Burt said, and they both started to laugh.

"Wait! Sometimes my mom leaves a house key in the car," Mullet said, sitting up.

The risk of walking through the neighborhood wearing girly sweatpants was worth it. They found a spare key to Mullet's house sitting in the glove box. Mullet held it up with exuberance.

"Nothing about this case makes sense. Do you think her mom is eating it and blaming her?" Mullet said as he opened the door and sat on the couch.

"No," Burt said, "She'd have to be evil to do that to her own daughter. She really believes that Darcy is lying to her and is punishing her to make her tell the truth."

"Yeah, I guess," Mullet said.

"I hope Darcy's not in too much trouble. I wonder what her mom is going to do to punish her now," Burt said.

"We can worry about it tomorrow, I'm getting too tired to think," Mullet said. He laid back down and started snoring.

Burt stared at the ceiling, feeling like he was never going to fall asleep.

—Chapter 17—
LEMONADE SALESMEN ...AGAIN

It was mid-morning before either of them woke up. Mullet's mom was already gone, but she left a note on the table along with several boxes of cereal.

Mullet sighed. "Being a detective is a lot harder than I thought it would be."

They'd just finished another box of cereal and were sitting on the couch, still tired from the night before. But not too tired to be out of Darcy's sweatpants and in the safety of their own basketball clothes.

"Maybe we were better off selling lemonade," Mullet said.

"We can't give up, not after we've been through so much. The answer has to be right in front of us," Burt said.

"Maybe we should just go sell lemonade. Maybe it will help us think of something we missed with the case. At least it's a steady income," Mullet said.

"Steady?" Burt said, "Maybe slow and steady…"

They ran over to Burt's house, made a pitcher of lemonade, and headed out to the drive. Their ideas to catch the peanut butter thief were more pitiful than their lemonade sales. No one came for lemonade all morning and no ideas came to their heads. Mostly they sat there and moped. Summer was ruined. Basketball stunk, their lemonade stand was slow, and the shoes on their feet were still wrapped with duct tape. The one real chance they had to make actual money was blown with one loud belch.

Burt took a sip of the lemonade that was too warm. The afternoon was hot and no one was going to be happy with lukewarm lemonade, not that there were any customers around to complain. They were worse salesmen than they were detectives.

Mullet's mom passed by Burt's driveway around four and they waved at her. She parked her car and walked over to them with a big smile on her face.

"You boys have been working so hard," she said.

Mullet looked at Burt.

"I am so proud that you two have been working to earn money yourselves. For that, I think I need to buy this pitcher of lemonade. I have nothing else to do tonight but sit on the porch and drink it," she said. She grabbed the pitcher off the table and dropped a five-dollar bill in its place.

Burt looked at Mullet. They both knew money was tight, and he had a thing about taking any money from his mom. Burt stood, but Mullet beat him to it, grabbed the bill, and chased his mom down.

"Mom, you don't have to do that," he said.

"Yeah, Mrs. Mullet, it's on the house for you, I mean think of all the food you feed us," Burt yelled from the table.

Somehow that made it even worse because then she beamed at them with such pride, that they didn't know what else to say. "Wow, what has happened to the boys I used to know? Not only are they responsible, but thoughtful on top of it. I think I can spare five dollars for some good lemonade. Consider it your lucky day," she said with a wink.

"Now I feel really guilty," Mullet finally said, "I don't know if we've been that responsible at all."

"But look how happy she was thinking that we are responsible. Sometimes it's the thought that counts," Burt said.

"Yeah, now I feel like I should clean my room or something," Mullet said. He didn't say anything and Burt knew he was probably thinking about his dad. It had been rough for them ever since he passed away, probably a lot harder than either of them let on.

"Maybe your mom is right and it will be our lucky day," Burt said, "It really can't get any worse than yesterday. Let's go make some more lemonade."

They decided to make more lemonade with lots of ice this time.

After they sat down, Burt poured himself a glass. "This is the life."

"If there isn't enough lemonade for customers I am going to pummel you," Mullet said.

"If any customers actually show up, I'll pummel myself for you," Burt said.

"No one's coming and no one is going to come. Maybe we'd be more productive practicing basketball or something," Mullet said.

"Nah, it's too hot for that. That's why they canceled tonight's practice," Burt said as he leaned back in his chair and held up his glass.

Mullet pulled out the copy of the DGB and flipped to the back of the book. He leaned over the page, becoming so engrossed with whatever he was reading about that he fell completely silent.

Burt scooted closer to Mullet to read over his shoulder.

As he moved over, he saw something out of the corner of his eye. He looked up as a group of people flew around the corner. He nudged Mullet. The group stopped and walked in from the walking path entrance. There were lots of grownups, all wearing athletic tops and running shorts. A lady stepped to the front of the group.

Mullet had already lost interest and was back to reading the DGB again.

"Hey, doesn't that lady look familiar?" Burt said, nudging him.

Mullet glanced up.

"Don't look so obvious," Burt said, "You know, tip number eight... a detective never looks obvious."

"I know that," Mullet said as he pretended to flip the page, but was actually studying the group. "Yeah, she does look familiar. They are coming this way. Maybe we'll recognize her closer up."

The group continued to walk and slowed as they approached the lemonade sign. The lady in the front of the group waved at them.

"Hi there, boys!" she said enthusiastically.

They glanced at each other. Mullet's face turned bright red. Standing in front of them was Darcy's Aunt Lizzie. She looked a little different with a bright red face, sweaty clothes, and messy hair.

She smiled reassuringly. "Hey there, no hard feelings about last night! I thought it was funny and I was glad to see Darcy with friends that she gets along with."

Burt exchanged a quick look with Mullet. He wouldn't exactly describe their relationship with Darcy as a friendship…and they definitely wouldn't say that they got along with her very well.

"So, you're selling lemonade? It looks nice and cold. I'll take some," she said as she fiddled with the pocket of her shorts. She dropped a sweaty dollar on the table and poured herself a glass. "Keep the change, it's a tip."

Burt started to protest, but she interrupted him.

"I won't hear it, besides, there is nothing better than cold lemonade after a long run. Believe me, it's worth a dollar," she said as she gulped it down.

She introduced the rest of her running group as the Red Pine Running Club and described Burt and Mullet as the midnight capers. The other runners bought lemonade, emptying their pitcher.

"Do you have any more?" a runner named Steve asked.

Burt nodded. "It's inside, I'll go get it."

As he ran into the garage to get the other batch of lemonade they'd mixed up, he heard Darcy's aunt say that she'd be right back. He hurried back out and gave all the runners refills.

"What are you saving your money for?" Steve asked.

"New basketball shoes," Mullet said.

"We know all about the importance of good shoes," Steve said as he plopped a few dollars on the table and poured some more lemonade.

The other runners agreed and added more change to the lemonade jar. Burt and Mullet tried to protest, but the runners just told them they were happy for their money to go to a good cause and to keep staying active.

Darcy's aunt returned. "Sorry guys, the door is locked. She normally keeps it open." She turned towards Burt and Mullet and waggled her finger, "I bet it's your fault I can't get in now. She doesn't want any stray boys sneaking into her house."

They both must have looked stricken with fear because she suddenly started laughing, "I was just teasing."

Burt relaxed, but only slightly, because he wasn't sure if she was really teasing or not. Mullet looked just as uncomfortable too.

"Oh well," she said as she turned back to her group, "Sorry guys, we aren't going to be able to get any protein here, but there's a little grocery store a block down the road where we can grab something to eat."

She turned to Burt and Mullet and explained that they were training for a marathon and needed protein for muscle recovery. "I run this way a few times a week and always stop at Darcy's house for a protein-rich snack to recharge after a long run. At least Hower's Grocery Store is just around the corner."

With that, she waved goodbye and the runners took off towards the grocery store.

Burt and Mullet stared at the mound of dollar bills and change piled on the table. Mullet's mom was right, it might actually be their lucky day. They were too excited to do anything except count their money. There were twelve one-dollar bills, two dollars in quarters, and the five-dollar bill from Mrs. Mullet. Counting what they made from Mullet's mom, they made nineteen dollars!

They turned and high-fived each other.

"Things couldn't be going better," Burt said as he stuffed the money into the jar.

"Except for the fact that we didn't catch the peanut butter thief," Mullet said.

"Yeah, we almost had a chance to get the thief and the shoes," Burt said as he closed the lid on the canning jar.

Mullet suddenly jumped up. "Wait a second!" He shouted. He bent down to put his shoes on and grabbed the canning jar away from Burt. Then he threw it in his mom's car and raced down the sidewalk.

"What are you doing?" Burt said, jumping to his feet.

"We need to get to Ben's store right now!" He yelled. He was already halfway down the sidewalk by the time Burt caught up with him.

"Why? What's going on?" Burt said through labored breaths as he chased Mullet down the sidewalk and around the corner.

"No time to explain," Mullet said as he ran at full speed down the road. "I'd give anything to have my backpack so I could get my binoculars out right now."

They sprinted down the next block, breathing heavily as sweat poured down their faces from the humid summer air. All Burt could think about was a nice cold glass of lemonade and the shady tree at the end of his driveway. He didn't know what Mullet was doing, but if he was still alive after this terrible run, he was going to get him good.

Mullet stopped across the road from Ben's store and ducked behind the blue post office box.

"I hope we aren't too late," Mullet whispered.

"Too late for what?" Burt said.

"Oh good! We aren't too late!" he said as he pointed at the door. "We aren't too late to catch our thief."

Burt looked up and watched the runners walk out the door. Steve was ripping open a package of protein bars. Someone else unpeeled a banana, and someone else guzzled down a protein drink. In the very back was Darcy's aunt, opening a jar of the store's really expensive peanut butter.

Burt's mouth dropped and he looked at Mullet. "No way."

"I think we better go talk to her and figure out for sure if she is the thief," Mullet said.

They looked both ways for traffic and hurried over to the group of runners.

"Wait!" Mullet said, stopping in the middle of the road, "The DGB says not to give yourself away to your suspects!"

"Whatever, Mullet," Burt said as he shoved him across the road.

—Chapter 18—
THE CONFESSION

Mullet chased after him as Burt waved down the runners.

Steve got Aunt Lizzie's attention and she walked over to them. "What's up, boys?" She scooped her spoon into the peanut butter and took a bite as she waited for their reply.

Burt suddenly became tongue-tied. He liked Aunt Lizzie and didn't want to accuse her of being a thief in front of all of her friends. He looked at Mullet, who looked just as hesitant to call her the peanut butter thief.

"Well, out with it," she said as she ate another bite of peanut butter and looked between both of them.

"We were just wondering if you normally stop at Darcy's house and eat peanut butter after you run," Burt finally said.

"Yes, I always do," she said with a smile, "But why would you want to know that?"

"The reason we were at Darcy's house last night was because she hired us to catch the peanut butter thief," Burt said.

Darcy's aunt looked confused.

"We're the local detectives," Mullet added. He pulled a detective badge out of the pocket of his pants and held it out to her.

She looked at it, but she still seemed confused, so Burt added, "Darcy was grounded for the entire summer because her mom, I mean, your sister, thought she was the one eating her expensive peanut butter and then lying about it. That's when Darcy hired us to solve the crime."

Darcy's aunt looked at the peanut butter jar in her hand, looked back at them, and started to laugh.

Burt and Mullet fidgeted uncomfortably. It wasn't as fun to catch the thief as they thought it would be, especially since it was Aunt Lizzie, and she was pretty nice. They thought the thief would be a real bad guy.

"So, I'm a thief, huh?" she said with a slight smile.

They nodded. "I'm afraid so," Burt said, feeling even worse.

"The sheriff's office is right over there, do you want to haul me in detectives?" she said, holding out her arms.

They both shook their heads and the rest of the runners all chuckled.

"Let me make sure that I have this straight. You're telling me that Darcy has been grounded for the entire summer because of me?" Aunt Lizzie said. She held up the peanut butter. "Because of this?"

They nodded again.

"Well, I will confess boys, you're pretty good little detectives. You caught me. I always stop in there to get water and peanut butter. It's my favorite running snack. I didn't think anything about it, because my sister told me to help myself to anything I wanted. I bet she forgot my favorite post-run protein is peanut butter. How about you go tell Darcy you cracked the case and I'll be over there shortly to explain," she said as she waved and took off with the other runners.

Mullet turned to Burt, his face turning bright red and looking like he was about to faint in the middle of the sidewalk.

Burt reached out to steady him. "Mullet, are you okay? What's wrong?" he said as he reached out to steady his friend.

"We solved it, we solved our very first crime!" he said as his eyes got really big. Suddenly his expression turned from shock to happiness. "We actually did it! We're real detectives! I printed fake badges, but they might as well be real!"

Burt grinned. "Yeah, we did. Especially thanks to your great thinking. I would have never put the two together."

"Good thing I read that book of facts about athletes last year. That's what finally made it click. You know what this means, right?" Mullet said.

"We get our shoes!" Burt said as they did their secret detective handshake. That wasn't in their guidebook, but it was a good addition.

They raced back to Darcy's house, ran up to her front porch, and punched her fancy doorbell.

Darcy's mom opened the door. When she saw it was them, she started to shut it.

"No, wait, Mrs. Bell," Burt said as he shoved his duct tape shoe between the door to stop it from closing. "We have something very important to tell you."

"I hope that it is an apology," she said as she crossed her arms.

"Well, we are sorry," Mullet said.

"But that isn't why we are here," Burt said.

It was a good thing looks couldn't actually kill or Mrs. Bell would be the death of a lot of kids, including them. No wonder Darcy was scared to death of getting in trouble.

Burt swallowed, remembering rule number three in their detective guide... A detective had to be brave.

"Mrs. Bell, the reason we were in your house last night was because we were on a stakeout. You see, Darcy hired us," Burt said.

"Hired you? What, for that ridiculous prank?"

"No, we're the local kid detectives," Mullet added as he pulled out the wadded badge and handed it to Darcy's mom. Little bits of lint stuck to the badge, and a yellow candy wrapper dangled from the bottom of it. "Oh, let me get that," Mullet said, reaching for the candy wrapper, "Wouldn't want it to go in the garbage disposal, or anything like that."

She looked disgusted, but luckily, she was still listening. "Continue on," she said.

"You see Mrs. Bell, we're Burt and Mullet, the local kid detectives," Burt said, "And we came to tell you that Darcy didn't steal your peanut butter. She's been telling the truth the entire time. She shouldn't be grounded the entire summer or miss her summer theater audition." He paused and waited.

"Of all the nerve," Mrs. Bell said through gritted teeth, "Did she put you up to this?" Her face became redder than Mullet's and contorted into something much scarier than all of the animals combined in the study. Her nostrils flared. "That child has taken this too far."

Just then, Darcy came down the stairs. She stopped when she saw the look on her mother's face and turned deathly white. No one said a word.

Finally, Burt leaned around her mom and gave her a thumbs up. "We solved the case."

"You did?" Darcy said, her face lighting up.

"We need to put an end to this ridiculous nonsense," Mrs. Bell said.

Thankfully, Aunt Lizzie pulled up in her car. Burt had never felt such relief. Hopefully, Mrs. Bell would believe her own sister. She stepped out of the car and reached into the back to wrangle a handful of balloons and a grocery bag out of the door.

Burt and Mullet ran over to help her. "She doesn't believe us," Burt whispered under his breath as Mrs. Bell marched out behind them.

"Odds are ten to one that she is going to murder us and there won't be any kid detectives left to solve any more neighborhood crimes," Mullet said.

"Don't worry, I got this," Aunt Lizzie said.

"Lizzie! You should hear this insane story these boys are telling me, something about detectives, and trying to get Darcy out of trouble for the summer," she said so harshly that Burt shuddered.

"It may sound like a crazy story, but they're right!" Aunt Lizzie said, "That's why I have these balloons. I owe little Miss Darcy a very big apology."

"What do you mean?" Mrs. Bell said.

Aunt Lizzie handed the grocery bag to Mrs. Bell. "Take a look in there."

Mrs. Bell uncurled the top of the paper bag and stared inside. She looked back at Aunt Lizzie. "It's a bag full of peanut butter."

"I'm the one that's been eating your peanut butter whenever I stop at your house after a run," she said, "Now, where is Darcy?"

Mrs. Bell's face turned from anger, to surprise, to something that looked downright grim.

"You mean, I've been mad at Darcy for no reason at all?" she said.

Everyone nodded.

"Oh dear," she said. She turned and hurried towards the porch, calling for Darcy.

Aunt Lizzie followed after her, the balloons bobbing up and down as they went.

Mullet turned to look at Burt. "What now?"

"I don't know. Maybe we should just go home," Burt said.

"Good idea," Mullet said as he whirled around to get out of there.

As they headed back to Burt's house, it seemed like there was nothing left to do. The case was solved, and it was too hot for basketball or to be outside for very long.

They paged through the guidebook, which didn't explain how boring life seemed after solving a big case. They finally decided to clean up their lemonade stand. As they trudged across the lawn, Burt noticed something shiny in the flowerbed around the tree. He leaned over. It was a bracelet.

"Hey, that must be Tiana's bracelet," Mullet said, "I bet it fell off the day she was getting lemonade."

"We better get this back to Tiana's house," Burt said as he turned to head down the street. When he looked up, he saw a girl in a blue dress and big bow coming towards them. "Here comes Darcy, I wonder what's going to happen now."

—Chapter 19—
CASE CLOSED

Something about the way she walked was a little strange and then he realized that she was carrying something big on her back.

"Look! Look at that," Mullet said, "She's got the backpack."

She shuffled forward slowly, like Mullet did when he wasn't feeling very confident. By the time she got to them, they almost had the lemonade stand packed up.

"I wanted to give you this," Darcy said as she held out the backpack. "And this too." In her hand was a white envelope. "Go ahead and open it."

Burt took the envelope and opened it, while Mullet peered over his shoulder. He had expected to see money, but it was only a white slip of paper. He looked up at her.

"Don't read it yet, and I know there's no money." Her eyes filled with tears. "My mom wouldn't let me give you my allowance. I'm really sorry. I tried to tell her how important it was and that you were saving for new shoes, but she wouldn't hear any of it."

Burt and Mullet looked at each other. A week ago, all they could think about was the shoes, but now they didn't seem as important anymore.

Darcy wiped her eyes.

"It's not a big deal. I mean, you've already had such a bad summer anyways. We wouldn't want to take anything else from you. Plus your aunt's running friends bought a bunch of lemonade," Burt said.

Suddenly Darcy reached up and hugged them both. "Just so you know, you really are great detectives… and the best friends I've ever had."

Neither of them had ever let a girl hug them, at least, a girl that wasn't family, and Burt was relieved when she let go. Also, they'd never imagined they could ever be friends with someone like Darcy. Not that they were necessarily great friends or anything, but somehow this case had brought them together.

"Don't forget to read that. I have to get to my play practice tonight thanks to you two," she said as she rushed off.

"Huh," Mullet said as he grabbed one corner of their lemonade stand.

"Huh, what?" Burt said.

"I mean, I know we just undestroyed her whole summer, but what about when we get back to school and all her friends start making fun of us?" he said.

"I don't know about school," Burt said, "But did you see that we've been invited to her house for a dinner party?"

"Oh right, the note. Let me see that," Mullet said as he yanked the white paper out of Burt's hand.

Burt held it away from him. Mullet lunged forward and they both toppled to the ground, wrestling for the white paper.

The door of Burt's front door opened. "Burt! Mullet!" Burt's mom yelled, "Get up here, I've just had a call from Mrs. Bell from down the road."

They looked at each other and their eyes grew wide. They made their way very slowly up the driveway, waiting for a lecture about their detective business.

"Listen," Burt's mom said, "She just called and said that you helped her daughter Darcy out. They've invited you to dinner tonight and said they had something special for you. Mullet, I already talked to your mom at work, and she said that was fine. I want you both to come in and get cleaned up."

At least they weren't in trouble. His mom could have put an end to their detective business right then and there.

"And," she said as she gave them "the look" that he always knew meant something bad was coming.

Uh oh. They were busted for sure.

"I would like to know why Mrs. Bell asked for you to bring Darcy's pink and purple sweatpants back. Did you take sweatpants from that poor girl?"

"We borrowed them," Burt said, looking at Mullet for help.

"Borrowed them or were you pranking her? Boys?"

"It was more like we were helping her with a prank," Mullet said.

"Interesting, because, when I heard this, I decided to call your mom Mullet. A few minutes later, she sent me a picture of the two of you." She pulled out her phone and held it out for them. There, lying on the couch, were the two of them sleeping in Darcy's too-tight pink and purple sweat suits. "Now, I expect the both of you to be on your best behavior for the rest of your lives… or else," she said with a grin as she waved her phone.

"Oh no," they both said in unison.

They started inside when Burt realized he still had Tiana's bracelet in his hand. He held it out to Mullet.

"We better return this first," Burt said.

Mullet raised his eyebrows.

"Let's just get it done and over with," he said.

"Okay," Mullet said.

They left their stuff and trudged over to Tiana's house. Mullet rang the doorbell and asked for her. A few minutes later, Tiana stepped out. Burt handed her the bracelet.

Her mouth dropped.

"Oh wow," she said, "You found it. I knew you were the greatest detectives. I knew it. I'm going to tell everyone about it."

Burt smiled. He definitely didn't doubt it.

"Wait here," she said as she ran back into her house. She came back and presented them each with a candy bar.

They thanked her and walked away. Mullet had a big grin on his face. He kept looking Burt's way and grinning until Burt couldn't stand it anymore.

"Okay, just say it," he said.

He smiled, "Can I have your wrapper when you're done?"

Burt unwrapped his candy bar and ate it, handing over the wrapper to Mullet who shoved it in his pocket.

"I am slowly getting my collection back," Mullet said, "You know, I kind of like tip number ninety-nine, a good detective always follows up."

Burt gave him a high-five. "And I like tip number one hundred, a good detective never gives up."

They realized they were still short of getting the shoes, but they didn't care as much. If they could be detectives and make a friend out of Darcy, then they could play in the tournament with any shoes, even duct-taped ones.

They cleaned themselves up for dinner at Darcy's. To their surprise, Darcy's entire family was there. Even better, dinner wasn't some stuffy thing in the dining room, but pizza around the kitchen island and a huge plate of peanut butter cookies.

After they finished, Darcy's mom handed them each an envelope. "Go ahead, open it."

Inside was a gift card to the sports store. They both looked up at her.

"I wouldn't let Darcy pay you because she never should have been in that position in the first place. This is our gift to you for helping fix everything. I already checked with both of your moms to make sure it was okay. Besides, I really don't want you over here again with those filthy duct tape shoes tromping through my house. Deal?"

"Deal!" they said as everyone laughed.

They spent the remainder of their evening in their headquarters studying about detectives. The number one rule in "The Detective's Guide to Being a Great Detective", also known as the DGB, is that a detective is always prepared. They were ready. The detective backpack hung on the wall, packed up, list checked twice, waiting for the next big case.

Keep an eye out for more adventures with
Burt and Mullet: Kid Detectives
Coming Soon!

Made in the USA
Monee, IL
10 October 2023